"You Can't Be Serious."

"I'm completely serious." Elliot's fingers twisted in Lucy Ann's ponytail.

"Let. Go. Now," she said, barely able to keep herself from hauling him in for a kiss. "Sex will only complicate matters."

"Or it could simplify things." He released her hair slowly, his stroke tantalizing all the way down her arm.

"Lucy Ann?" His bourbon-smooth tones intoxicated her parched senses. "What are you thinking?"

"My aunt said the same thing about the bonus of friends becoming...more."

He laughed softly, the heat of his breath broadcasting how close he'd moved to her. "Your aunt has always been a smart woman. Although, I sure as hell didn't talk to her about you and I becoming lovers."

"You need to quit saying things like that. You and I need boundaries for this to work."

His gaze fell to her mouth for an instant that stretched to eternity. "We'll have to agree to disagree."

* * *

For the Sake of Their Son
is part of The Alpha Brotherhood series:
Bound by an oath to make amends,
these billionaires can conquer anything...but love.

Twitter,
f Harlequin Desire!
desire

Dear Reader,

Thank you for picking up book five in my Alpha Brotherhood series! For those of you who may be new to this special breed of heroes, each book can be read as a standalone. Or you can order the first four: *An Inconvenient Affair, All or Nothing, Playing for Keeps* and *Yuletide Baby Surprise.*

In *For the Sake of Their Son,* I was intrigued by the notion of just how much a mother would do for her child. As the mother of four, I know I would do just about anything for mine. Lucky for the hero and heroine, Elliot and Lucy Ann, their infant son helps them find their own path to happily ever after!

Cheers!
Catherine Mann

www.CatherineMann.com

www.Facebook.com/CatherineMannAuthor

www.Twitter.com/CatherineMann1

FOR THE SAKE
OF THEIR SON

—

CATHERINE MANN

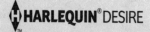

Recycling programs
for this product may
not exist in your area.

ISBN-13: 978-0-373-73288-3

FOR THE SAKE OF THEIR SON

Copyright © 2014 by Catherine Mann

Printed in U.S.A.

CATHERINE MANN

USA TODAY bestselling author Catherine Mann lives on a sunny Florida beach with her flyboy husband and their four children. With more than forty books in print in over twenty countries, she has also celebrated wins for both a RITA® Award and a Booksellers' Best Award. Catherine enjoys chatting with readers online—thanks to the wonders of the internet, which allows her to network with her laptop by the water! Contact Catherine through her website, www.catherinemann.com, find her on Facebook and Twitter (@CatherineMann1) or reach her by snail mail at P.O. Box 6065, Navarre, FL 32566.

For my children.

One

Elliot Starc had faced danger his whole life. First at the hands of his heavy-fisted father. Later as a Formula One race car driver who used his world travels to feed information to Interpol.

But he'd never expected to be kidnapped. Especially not in the middle of his best friend's bachelor party.

Mad as hell, Elliot struggled back to consciousness, only to realize his wrists were cuffed. Numb. He struggled against the restraints while trying to get his bearings, but his brain was still disoriented. Last he remembered, he'd been in Atlanta, Georgia, at a bachelor party and now he was cuffed and blindfolded, for God's sake. What the hell? He only knew that he was in the back of a vehicle that smelled of leather and luxury. Noise offered him little to go on. Just the purr of a finely tuned engine. The pop of an opening soda can. A low hum of music so faint it must be on a headset.

"He's awake," a deep voice whispered softly, too softly to be identified.

"Damn it," another voice hissed.

"Hey," Elliot shouted, except it wasn't a shout. More of a hoarse croak. He cleared his throat and tried again. "Whatever the hell is going on here, we can talk ransom—"

A long buzz sounded. Unmistakable. The closing of a privacy window. Then silence. Solitude, no chance of shouting jack to anyone in this...

A limo, perhaps? Who kidnapped someone using a limousine?

Once they stopped, he would be ready, though. The second he could see, he wouldn't even need his hands. He was trained in seven different forms of self-defense. He could use his feet, his shoulders and his body weight.

He would be damned before he let himself ever be helpless in a fight.

They'd pulled off an interstate at least twenty minutes ago, driving into the country as best he could tell. He had no way of judging north, south or west. He could be anywhere from Florida to Mississippi to South Carolina, and God knows he had enemies in every part of the world from his work with Interpol and his triumphs over competitors in the racing world.

And he had plenty of pissed-off ex-girlfriends.... He winced at the thought of females and Carolina so close together. Home. Too many memories. Bad ones—with just a single bright spot in the form of Lucy Ann Joyner, but he'd wrecked even that.

Crap.

Back to the present. Sunlight was just beginning to filter through the blindfold, sparking behind his eyes like shards of glinting glass.

One thing was certain. This car had good shock absorbers. Otherwise the rutted road they were traveling would have rattled his teeth.

Although his teeth were clenched mighty damn tight right now.

Even now, he still couldn't figure out how he'd been blindsided near the end of Rowan Boothe's bachelor party in an Atlanta casino. Elliot had ducked into the back to find a vintage Scotch. Before he could wrap his hand around the neck of the bottle, someone had knocked him out.

If only he knew the motive for his kidnapping. Was someone after his money? Or had someone uncovered his secret dealings with Interpol? If so, did they plan to exploit that connection?

He'd lived his life to the fullest, determined to do better than his wrong-side-of-the-tracks upbringing. He only had one regret: how his lifelong friendship with Lucy Ann had crashed and burned more fiercely than when he'd been sideswiped at the Australian Grand Prix last year—

The car jerked to a halt. He braced his feet to keep from rolling off onto the floor. He forced himself to stay relaxed so his abductors would think he was still asleep.

His muscles tensed for action, eager for the opportunity to confront his adversaries. Ready to pay back. He was trained from his work with Interpol, with lightning-fast instincts honed in his racing career. He wouldn't go down without a fight.

Since he'd left his dirt-poor roots behind, he'd been beating the odds. He'd dodged juvie by landing in a military reform school where he'd connected with a lifelong group of friends. Misfits like himself who disdained rules while living by a strict code of justice. They'd grown up to take different life paths, but stayed connected through their friendship and freelance work for Interpol. Not that they'd been much help to him while someone was nabbing him a few feet away from the bachelor party they were all attending.

The car door opened and someone leaned over him. Something tugged at the back of his brain, a sense that he should know this person. He scrambled to untangle the mystery before it was too late.

His blindfold was tugged up and off, and he took in the inside of a black limo, just as he'd suspected. His abductors, however, were a total surprise.

"Hello, Elliot, my man," said his old high school pal Malcolm Douglas, who'd asked him to fetch that bottle of Scotch back at the bachelor party. "Waking up okay?"

Conrad Hughes—another traitorous bastard friend— patted his face. "You look plenty awake to me."

Elliot bit back a curse. He'd been kidnapped by his own comrades from the bachelor party. "Somebody want to tell me what's going on here?"

He eyed Conrad and Malcolm, both of whom had been living it up with him at the casino well past midnight. Morning sunshine streamed over them, oak trees sprawling behind them. The scent of Carolina jasmine carried on the breeze. Why were they taking him on this strange road trip?

"Well?" he pressed again when neither of them answered. "What the hell are you two up to?" he asked, his anger barely contained. He wanted to kick their asses. "I hope you have a good reason for taking me out to the middle of nowhere."

Conrad clapped him on the back. "You'll see soon enough."

Elliot angled out of the car, hard as hell with his hands

cuffed in front of him. His loafers hit the dirt road, rocks and dust shifting under his feet as he stood in the middle of nowhere in a dense forest of pines and oaks. "You'll tell me now or I'll beat the crap out of both of you."

Malcolm lounged against the side of the black stretch limo. "Good luck trying with your hands cuffed. Keep talking like that and we'll hang on to the key for a good long while."

"Ha—funny—not." Elliot ground his teeth in frustration. "Isn't it supposed to be the groom who gets pranked?"

Conrad grinned. "Oh, don't worry. Rowan should be waking up and finding his new tattoo right about now."

Extending his cuffed wrists, Elliot asked, "And the reason for this? I'm not the one getting married."

Ever.

Malcolm pushed away, jerking his head to the side, gesturing toward the path leading into the dense cluster of more pine trees with an occasional magnolia reaching for the sun. "Instead of telling you why, we'll just let you look. Walk with us."

As if he had any choice. His friends clearly had some kind of game planned and they intended to see it through regardless. Sure, he'd been in a bear of a mood since his breakup with Gianna. Hell, even before that. Since Lucy Ann had quit her job as his assistant and walked out of his life for good.

God, he really needed to pour out some frustration behind the wheel, full out, racing to…anywhere.

A few steps deeper into the woods, his blood hummed with recognition. The land was more mature than the last time he'd been here, but he knew the area well enough. Home. Or rather it used to be home, back when he was a poor kid with a drunken father. This small South Carolina farm town outside of Columbia had been called God's land.

Elliot considered it a corner of hell.

Although hell was brimming with sunshine today.

He stepped toward a clearing and onto a familiar dirt driveway, with a ranch-style cabin and a fat oak at least a hundred years old in the middle. A tree he'd played under as a kid, wishing he could stay here forever because this little haven in hell was a lot safer than his home.

He'd hidden with Lucy Ann Joyner here at her aunt's farmhouse. Both of them enjoying the sanctuary of this place, even if only for a few hours. Why were his buds taking him down this memory lane detour?

Branches rustled, a creaking sound carrying on the breeze, drawing his gaze. A swing dangled from a thick branch, moving back and forth as a woman swayed, her back to them. He stopped cold. Suddenly the meaning of this journey was crystal clear. His friends were forcing a confrontation eleven months in the making since he and Lucy Ann were both too stubborn to take the first step.

Did she know he was coming? He swallowed hard at the notion that maybe she wanted him here after all. That her decision to slice him out of her life had changed. But if she had, then why not just drive up to the house?

He wasn't sure the past year could be that easily forgotten, but his gut twisted tight over just the thought of talking to her again.

His eyes soaked in the sight of her, taking her in like parched earth with water. He stared at the slim feminine back, the light brown hair swishing just past her shoulders. Damn, but it had been a long eleven months without her. His lifelong pal had bolted after one reckless— incredible—night that had ruined their friendship forever.

He'd given her space and still hadn't heard from her.

In the span of a day, the one person he'd trusted above everyone else had cut him off. He'd never let anyone get that close to him—not even his friends from the military reform school. He and Lucy Ann had a history, a shared link that went beyond a regular friendship.

Or so he'd thought.

As if drawn by a magnet, he walked closer to the swing, to the woman. His hands still linked in front of him, he moved silently, watching her. The bared lines of her throat evoked memories of her jasmine scent. The way her dress slipped ever so slightly off one shoulder reminded him of years past when she'd worn hand-me-downs from neighbors.

The rope tugged at the branch as she toe-tapped, back and forth. A gust of wind turned the swing spinning to face him.

His feet stumbled to a halt.

Yes, it was Lucy Ann, but not just her. Lucy Ann stared back at him with wide eyes, shocked eyes. She'd clearly been kept every bit as much in the dark as he had. Before he could finish processing his disappointment that she hadn't helped arrange this, his eyes took in the biggest shocker of all.

Lucy Ann's arms were curved around an infant swaddled in a blue plaid blanket as she breast-fed him.

Lucy Ann clutched her baby boy to her chest and stared in shock at Elliot Starc, her childhood friend, her former boss. Her onetime lover.

The father of her child.

She'd scripted the moment she would tell him about their son a million times in her mind, but never had it played out like this, with him showing up out of the blue. Handcuffed? Clearly, he hadn't planned on coming to see her. She'd tempted fate in waiting so long to tell him, then he'd pulled one of his disappearing acts and she couldn't find him.

Now there was no avoiding him.

Part of her ached to run to Elliot and trust in the friendship they'd once shared, a friendship built here, in the wooded farmland outside Columbia, South Carolina. But another part of her—the part that saw his two friends lurking and the handcuffs on her old pal—told her all she needed to know. Elliot hadn't suddenly seen the light and come running to apologize for being a first-class jerk. He'd been dragged kicking and screaming.

Well, screw him. She had her pride, too.

Only the baby in her arms kept her from bolting altogether into her aunt's cabin up the hill. Lucy Ann eased Eli from her breast and adjusted her clothes in place. Shifting her son to her shoulder, she patted his back, her eyes staying locked on Elliot, trying to gauge his mood.

The way his eyes narrowed told her loud and clear that she couldn't delay her explanation any longer. She should have told him about Eli sooner. In the early days of her pregnancy, she'd tried and chickened out. Then she'd gotten angry over his speedy rebound engagement to the goddess Gianna, and that made it easier to keep her distance a while longer. She wouldn't be the cause of breaking up his engagement—rat bastard. She would tell him once he was married and wouldn't feel obligated to offer her anything. Even though the thought of him marrying that too-perfect bombshell heiress made her vaguely nauseous.

Now, Elliot was here, so damn tall and muscular, his sandy brown hair closely shorn. His shoulders filled out the black button-down shirt, his jeans slung low on his hips. His five o'clock shadow and narrowed green eyes gave him a bad-boy air he'd worked his whole life to live up to.

She knew every inch of him, down to a scar on his elbow he'd told everyone he got from falling off his bike but he'd really gotten from the buckle on his father's belt during a beating. They shared so much history, and now they shared a child.

Standing, she pulled her gaze from him and focused on his old boarding school friends behind him, brooding Conrad Hughes and charmer Malcolm Douglas. Of course they'd dragged him here. These days both of them had sunk so deep into a pool of marital bliss, they seemed to think everyone else wanted to plunge in headfirst. No doubt they'd brought Elliot here with just that in mind.

Not a freakin' chance.

She wasn't even interested in dipping her toes into those waters and certainly not with Elliot, the biggest playboy in the free world.

"Gentlemen, do you think you could uncuff him, then leave so he and I can talk civilly?"

Conrad—a casino owner—fished out a key from his pocket and held it up. "Can do." He looked at Elliot. "I trust you're not going to do anything stupid like try to start a fight over our little prank here."

Prank? This was her life and they were playing with it. Anger sparked in her veins.

Elliot pulled a tight smile. "Of course not. I'm out-numbered. Now just undo the handcuffs. My arms are too numb to hit either of you anyway."

Malcolm plucked the keys from Conrad and opened the cuffs. Elliot massaged his wrists for a moment, still silent, then stretched his arms over his head.

Did he have to keep getting hotter every year? Especially not fair when she hadn't even had time to shower since yesterday thanks to her son's erratic sleeping schedule.

Moistening her dry mouth, Lucy Ann searched for a way to dispel the awkward air. "Malcolm, Conrad, I realize you meant well with this, but perhaps it's time for you both to leave. Elliot and I clearly have some things to discuss."

Eli burped. Lucy Ann rolled her eyes and cradled her son in the crook of her arm, too aware of the weight of Elliot's stare.

Malcolm thumped Elliot on the back. "You can thank us later."

Conrad leveled a somber steady look her way. "Call if you need anything. I mean that."

Without another word, both men disappeared back into the wooded perimeter as quickly as they'd arrived. For the first time in eleven months, she was alone with Elliot.

Well, not totally alone. She clutched Eli closer until he squirmed.

Elliot stuffed his hands in his pockets, still keeping his distance. "How long have you been staying with your aunt?"

"Since I left Monte Carlo." She'd been here the whole time, if he'd only bothered to look. Where else would she go? She had money saved up, but staying here made the most sense economically.

"How are you supporting yourself?"

"That's not your business." She lifted her chin. He had the ability to find out anything he wanted to know about her if he'd just looked, thanks to his Interpol connections.

Apparently, he hadn't even bothered to try. And that's what hurt the most. All these months, she'd thought he would check up on her. He would have seen she was pregnant. He would have wondered.

He would have come.

"Not my business?" He stalked a step closer, only a hint of anger showing in his carefully guarded eyes. "Really? I think we both know why it is so very much my business."

"I have plenty saved up from my years working for you." He'd insisted on paying her an outlandish salary to be his personal assistant. "And I'm doing virtual work to subsidize my income. I build and maintain websites. I make enough to get by." Her patience ran out with this small talk, the avoidance of discussing the baby sleeping in her arms. "You've had months to ask these questions and chose to remain silent. If anyone has a right to be angry, it's me."

"You didn't call either, and you have a much more compelling reason to communicate." He nodded toward Eli. "He is mine."

"You sound sure."

"I know you. I see the truth in your eyes," he said simply.

She couldn't argue with that. She swallowed once, twice, to clear her throat and gather her nerve. "His name is Eli. And yes, he's your son, two months old."

Elliot pulled his hands from his pockets. "I want to hold him."

Her stomach leaped into her throat. She'd envisioned this moment so many times, but living in it? She never could have imagined how deeply the emotions would rattle her. She passed over Eli to his father, watching Elliot's face. For once, she couldn't read him at all. So strange, considering how they'd once been so in sync they could finish each other's sentences, read a thought from a glance across a room.

Now, he was like a stranger.

Face a blank slate, Elliot held their son in broad, capable hands, palmed the baby's bottom and head as he studied the tiny cherub features. Eli still wore his blue footed sleeper from bedtime, his blond hair glistening as the sun sent dappled rays through the branches. The moment looked like a fairy tale, but felt so far from that her heart broke over how this should have, could have been.

Finally, Elliot looked up at her, his blasé mask sliding away to reveal eyes filled with ragged pain. His throat moved in a slow gulp of emotion. "Why did you keep this—Eli—from me?"

Guilt and frustration gnawed at her. She'd tried to contact him but knew she hadn't tried hard enough. Her pride... Damn it all. Her excuses all sounded weak now, even to her own ears.

"You were engaged to someone else. I didn't want to interfere in that."

"You never intended to tell me at all?" His voice went hoarse with disbelief, his eyes shooting back down to his son sleeping against his chest so contentedly as if he'd been there all along.

"Of course I planned to explain—after you were married." She dried her damp palms on her sundress. "I refused to be responsible for breaking up your great love match."

Okay, she couldn't keep the cynicism out of that last part, but he deserved it for his rebound relationship.

"My engagement to Gianna ended months ago. Why didn't you contact me?"

He had a point there. She ached to run, but he had her son. And as much as she hated to admit it to herself, she'd missed Elliot. They'd been so much a part of each other's lives for so long. The past months apart had been like a kind of withdrawal.

"Half the time I couldn't find you and the other half, your new personal secretary couldn't figure out where you were." And hadn't that pissed her off something fierce? Then worried her, because she knew about his sporadic missions for Interpol, and she also knew his reckless spirit.

"You can't have tried very hard, Lucy Ann. All you had to do was speak with any of my friends." His eyes narrowed. "Or did you? Is that why they brought me here today, because you reached out to them?"

She'd considered doing just that many times, only to balk at the last second. She wouldn't be manipulative. She'd planned to tell him face-to-face. And soon.

"I wish I could say yes, but I'm afraid not. One of them must have been checking up on me even if you never saw the need."

Oops. Where had that bitter jab come from?

He cocked an eyebrow. "This is about Eli. Not about the two of us."

"There is no 'two of us' anymore." She touched her son's head lightly, aching to take him back in her arms. "You ended that when you ran away scared after we had a reckless night of sex."

"I do *not* run away."

"Excuse me if your almighty ego is bruised." She crossed her arms over her chest, feeling as though they were in fifth grade again, arguing over whether the basketball was in or out of bounds.

Elliot sighed, looking around at the empty clearing. The limo's engine roared to life, then faded as it drove away without him. He turned back to Lucy Ann. "This isn't accomplishing anything. We need to talk reasonably about our child's future."

"I agree." Of course they had to talk, but right now her

heart was in her throat. She could barely think straight. She scooped her baby from his arms. "We'll talk tomorrow when we're both less rattled."

"How do I know you won't just disappear with my son?" He let go of Eli with obvious reluctance.

His son.

Already his voice echoed with possessiveness.

She clasped her son closer, breathing in the powder-fresh familiarity of him, the soft skin of his cheek pressed against her neck reassuringly. She could and she would manage her feelings for Elliot. Nothing and no one could be allowed to interfere with her child's future.

"I've been here all this time, Elliot. You just never chose to look." A bitter pill to swallow. She gestured up the empty dirt road. "Even now, you didn't choose. Your friends dumped you here on my doorstep."

Elliot walked a slow circle around her, his hand snagging the rope holding the swing until he stopped beside her. He had a way of moving with such fluidity, every step controlled, a strange contradiction in a man who always lived on the edge. Always flirting with chaos.

Her skin tingled to life with the memory of his touch, the wind teasing her with a hint of aftershave and musk.

She cleared her throat. "Elliot, I really think you should—"

"Lucy Ann," he interrupted, "in case it's escaped your notice, my friends left me here. Alone. No car." He leaned in closer, his hand still holding the rope for balance, so close she could almost feel the rasp of his five o'clock shadow. "So regardless of whether or not we talk, for now, you're stuck with me."

Two

Elliot held himself completely still, a feat of supreme control given the frustration racing through his veins. That Lucy Ann had hidden her pregnancy—his son—from him all this time threatened to send him to his knees. Somehow during this past year he'd never let go of the notion that everything would simply return to the way things had been before with them. Their friendship had carried him through the worst times of his life.

Now he knew there was no going back. Things between them had changed irrevocably.

They had a child together, a boy just inches away. Elliot clenched his hand around the rope. He needed to bide his time and proceed with caution. His lifelong friend had a million great qualities—but she was also stubborn as hell. A wrong step during this surprise meeting could have her digging in her heels.

He had to control his frustration, tamp down the anger

over all that she'd hidden from him. Staying levelheaded saved his life on more than one occasion on the racetrack. But never had the stakes been more important than now. No matter how robbed he felt, he couldn't let that show.

Life had taught him well how to hide his darker emotions.

So he waited, watching her face for some sign. The breeze lifted a strand of her hair, whipping it over his cheek. His pulse thumped harder.

"Well, Lucy Ann? What now?"

Her pupils widened in her golden-brown eyes, betraying her answering awareness a second before she bolted up from the swing. Elliot lurched forward as the swing freed. He released the rope and found his footing.

Lucy Ann glanced over her shoulder as she made her way to the graveled path. "Let's go inside."

"Where's your aunt?" He followed her, rocks crunching under his feet.

"At work." Lucy Ann walked up the steps leading to the prefab log cabin's long front porch. Time had worn the redwood look down to a rusty hue. "She still waits tables at the Pizza Shack."

"You used to send her money." He'd stumbled across the bank transaction by accident. Or maybe his accountant had made a point of letting him discover the transfers since Lucy Ann left so little for herself.

"Well, come to find out, Aunt Carla never used it," Lucy Ann said wryly, pushing the door open into the living room. The decor hadn't changed, the same brown plaid sofa with the same saggy middle, the same dusty Hummel figurines packed in a corner cabinet. He'd forgotten how Carla scoured yard sales religiously for the things, unable to afford them new.

They'd hidden here more than once as kids, then as

teenagers, plotting a way to escape their home lives. He eyed the son he'd barely met but who already filled his every plan going forward. "Your aunt's prideful, just like you."

"I accepted a job from you." She settled Eli into a portable crib by the couch.

"You worked your butt off and got your degree in computer technology." He admired the way she never took the easy way out. How she'd found a career for herself.

So why had she avoided talking to him? Surely not from any fear of confrontation. Her hair swung forward as she leaned into the baby crib, her dress clinging to her hips. His gaze hitched on the new curves.

Lucy Ann spun away from the crib and faced him again. "Are we going to keep making small talk or are you going to call a cab? I could drive you back into town."

"I'm not going anywhere."

Her eyebrows pinched together. "I thought we agreed to talk tomorrow."

"You decided. I never agreed." He dropped to sit on the sofa arm. If he sat in the middle, no telling how deep that sag would sink.

"You led me to believe…" She looked around as if searching for answers, but the Hummels stayed silent. "Damn it. You just wanted to get in the house."

Guilty as charged. "This really is the best place to discuss the future. Anywhere else and I'll have to be on the lookout for fans. We're in NASCAR country, you know. Not Formula One, but kissing cousins." He held up his hands. "Besides, my jackass buddies stranded me without my wallet."

She gasped. "You're joking."

"I wish." They must have taken it from his pocket while he was knocked out. He tamped down another surge of anger over being manipulated. If he'd just had some warning…

"Why did they do this to you—to both of us?" She sat on the other arm of the sofa, the worn width between them.

"Probably because they know how stubborn we are." He watched her face, trying to read the truth in the delicate lines, but he saw only exhaustion and dark circles. "Would you have ever told me about the baby?"

"You've asked me that already and I've answered. Of course I would have told you—" she shrugged "—eventually."

Finally he asked the question that had been plaguing him most. "How can I be sure?"

Shaking her head, she shrugged again. "You can't. You'll just have to trust me."

A wry smile tugged the corner of his mouth. "Trust has never been easy for either of us." But now that he was here and saw the truth, his decision was simple. "I want you and Eli to come with me, just for a few weeks while we make plans for the future."

"No." She crossed her arms over her chest.

"Ah, come on, Lucy Ann. Think about my request before you react."

"Okay. Thinking…" She tapped her temple, tapping, tapping. Her hand fell to her lap. "Still no."

God, her humor and spunk had lifted him out of hell so many times. He'd missed her since she'd stormed out of his life….

But he'd also missed out on a lot more in not knowing about his son.

"I can never regain those first two months of Eli's life." A bitter pill he wasn't sure how to swallow down. "I need a chance to make up for that."

She shook her head slowly. "You can't be serious about taking a baby on the road."

"I'm dead serious." He wasn't leaving here without them. He couldn't just toss money down and go.

"Let me spell it out for you then. Elliot, this is the middle of your racing season." She spoke slowly, as she'd done when they were kids and she'd tutored him in multiplication tables. "You'll be traveling, working, running with a party crowd. I've seen it year after year, enough to know that's no environment for a baby."

And damn it, she was every bit as astute now as she'd been then. He lined up an argument, a way to bypass her concerns. "You saw my life when there wasn't a baby around—no kids around, actually. It *can* be different. *I* can be different, like other guys who bring their families on the circuit with them." He shifted to sit beside her. "I have a damn compelling reason to make changes in my life. This is the chance to show you that."

Twisting the skirt of her dress in nervous fingers, she studied him with her golden-brown gaze for so long he thought he'd won.

Then resolve hardened her eyes again. "Expecting someone to change only sets us both up for disappointment."

"Then you'll get to say 'I told you so.' You told me often enough in the past." He rested a hand on top of hers to still the nervous fidgeting, squeezing lightly. "The best that happens is I'm right and this works. We find a plan to be good parents to Eli even when we're jet-setting around the world. Remember how much fun we used to have together? I miss you, Lucy Ann."

He thumbed the inside of her wrist, measuring the speed of her pulse, the softness of her skin. He'd done everything he could to put her out of his mind, but with no luck. He'd been unfair to Gianna, leading her to think he was free. So many regrets. He was tired of them. "Lucy Ann…"

She yanked her hand free. "Stop it, Elliot. I've watched you seduce a lot of women over the years. Your games don't work with me. So don't even try the slick moves."

"You wound me." He clamped a hand over his heart in an attempt at melodrama to cover his disappointment.

She snorted. "Hardly. You don't fool me with the pained look. It's eleven months too late to be genuine."

"You would be wrong about that."

"No games." She shot to her feet. "We both need time to regroup and think. We need to continue this conversation later."

"Fair enough then." He sat on the sofa, stretching both arms out along the back.

She stomped her foot. "What are you doing?"

He picked up the remote from the coffee table and leaned back again into the deepest, saggiest part. "Making myself comfortable."

"For what?"

He thumbed on the television. "If I'm going to stick around until you're ready to talk, I might as well scout the good stations. Any beer in the fridge? Although wait, it's too early for that. How about coffee?"

"No." She snatched the remote control from his hand. "And stop it. I don't know what game you're playing but you can quit and *go*. In case that wasn't clear enough, leave and come back later. You can take my car."

He took the remote right back and channel surfed without looking away from the flat screen. "Thanks for the generous offer of transportation, but you said we can't take Eli on the road and I only just met my son. I'm not leaving him now. How about the coffee?"

"Like hell."

"I don't need cream. Black will do just fine."

"Argh!" She slumped against the archway between the living room and kitchen. "Quit being ridiculous about the coffee. You know you're not staying here."

He set aside the remote, smiling as some morning talk show droned in the background. "So you'll come with me after all. Good."

"You're crazy. You know that, right?"

"No newsflash there, sweetheart. A few too many concussions." He stood. "Forget the suitcase."

"Run that by me again?"

"Don't bother with packing. I'll buy everything you need, everything new. Let's just grab a couple of diapers for the rug rat and go."

Her acceptance was becoming more and more important by the second. He needed her with him. He had to figure out a way to tie their lives together again so his son would know a father, a mother and a normal life.

"Stop! Stop trying to control my life." She stared at him sadly. "Elliot, I appreciate all you did for me in the past, but I don't need rescuing anymore."

"Last time I checked, I wasn't offering a rescue. Just a partnership."

If humor and pigheadedness didn't work, time to go back to other tactics. No great hardship really, since the attraction crackled between them every bit as tangibly now as it had the night they'd impulsively landed in bed together after a successful win. He sauntered closer. "As I recall, last time we were together, we shared control quite…nicely. And now that I think of it, we really don't need those clothes after all."

* * *

The rough upholstery of the sofa rasped against the backs of Lucy Ann's legs, her skin oversensitive, tingling to life after just a few words from Elliot. Damn it, she refused to be seduced by him again. The way her body betrayed her infuriated her down to her toes, which curled in her sandals.

Sure, he was beach-boy handsome, mesmerizingly sexy and blindingly charming. Women around the world could attest to his allure. However, in spite of her one unforgettable moment of weakness, she refused to be one of those fawning females throwing themselves at his feet.

No matter how deeply her body betrayed her every time he walked in the room.

She shot from the sofa, pacing restlessly since she couldn't bring herself to leave her son alone, even though he slept. Damn Elliot and the draw of attraction that had plagued her since the day they'd gone skinny-dipping at fourteen and she realized they weren't kids anymore.

Shutting off those thoughts, she pivoted on the coarse shag carpet to face him. "This is not the time or the place for sexual innuendo."

"Honey—" his arms stretched along the back of the sofa "—it's never a bad time for sensuality. For nuances. For seduction."

The humor in his eyes took the edge of arrogance off his words. "If you're aiming to persuade me to leave with you, you're going about it completely the wrong way."

"There's no denying we slept together."

"Clearly." She nodded toward the Pack 'n Play where their son slept contentedly, unaware that his little world had just been turned upside down.

"There's no denying that it was good between us. Very good."

Elliot's husky words snapped her attention back to his face. There wasn't a hint of humor in sight. Awareness tingled to the roots of her hair.

Swallowing hard, she sank into an old cane rocker. "It was impulsive. We were both tipsy and sentimental and reckless." The rush of that evening sang through her memory, the celebration of his win, reminiscing about his first dirt track race, a little wine, too much whimsy, then far too few clothes…. "I refuse to regret that night or call our…encounter…a mistake since I have Eli. But I do not intend to repeat the experience."

"Now that's just a damn shame. What a waste of good sexual chemistry."

"Will you please stop?" Her hands fisted on the arms of the wooden rocker. "We got along just fine as friends for thirty years."

"Are you saying we can be friends again?" He leaned forward, elbows on his knees. "No more hiding out and keeping big fat secrets from each other?"

His words carried too much truth for comfort. "You're twisting my words around."

"God's honest truth, Lucy Ann." He sighed. "I'm trying to call a truce so we can figure out how to plan our son's future."

"By telling me to ditch my clothes? You obviously missed class the day they taught the definition of truce."

"Okay, you're right. That wasn't fair of me." He thrust his hands through his hair. "I'm not thinking as clearly as I would like. Learning about Eli has been a shock to say the least."

"I can understand that." Her hands unfurled to grip the rocker. "And I am so very sorry for any pain this has caused you."

"Given that I've lost the first two months of my son's

life, the least you can do is give me four weeks together. Since you're working from home here, you'll be able to work on the road, as well. But if going on the race circuit is a deal breaker, I'll bow out this season."

She jolted in surprise that he would risk all he'd worked so hard to achieve, a career he so deeply loved. "What about your sponsors? Your reputation?"

"This is your call."

"That's not fair to make an ultimatum like that, to put it on me."

"I'm asking, and I'm offering you choices."

Choices? Hardly. She knew how important his racing career was to him. And she couldn't help but admit to feeling a bit of pride in having helped him along the way. There was no way she could let him back out now.

She tossed up her hands. "Fine. Eli and I will travel with you on the race circuit for the next four weeks so you can figure out whatever it is you want to know and make your plans. You win. You always do."

Winning didn't feel much like a victory tonight.

Elliot poured himself a drink from the wet bar at his hotel. He and Lucy Ann had struck a bargain that he would stay at a nearby historic home that had been converted into a hotel while she made arrangements to leave in the morning. He'd called for a car service to pick him up, making use of his credit card numbers, memorized, a fact he hadn't bothered mentioning to Lucy Ann earlier. Although she should have known. Had she selectively forgotten or had she been that rattled?

The half hour waiting for the car had been spent silently staring at his son while Eli slept and Lucy Ann hid in the other room under the guise of packing.

Elliot's head was still reeling. He had been knocked

unconscious and kidnapped, and found out he had an unknown son all in one day. He tipped back the glass of bourbon, emptying it and pouring another to savor, more slowly, while he sat out on the garden balcony where he would get better cell phone reception.

He dropped into a wrought-iron chair and let the Carolina moon pour over him. His home state brought such a mix of happy and sad memories. He was always better served just staying the hell away. He tugged his cell from his waistband, tucked his Bluetooth in his ear and thumbed autodial three for Malcolm Douglas.

The ringing stopped two buzzes in. "Brother, how's it going?"

"How do you think it's going, Douglas? My head hurts and I'm pissed off." Anger was stoked back to life just thinking about his friends' arrogant stunt, the way they'd played with his life. "You could have just told me about the baby."

Malcolm chuckled softly. "Wouldn't have been half as fun that way."

"Fun? You think this is some kind of game? You're a sick bastard." The thought of them plotting this out while he partied blissfully unaware had him working hard to keep his breath steady. He and his friends had played some harsh jokes on one another in the past, but nothing like this. "How long have you known?"

"For about a week," the chart-topping musician answered unrepentantly.

"A week." Seven days he could have had with his son. Seven days his best friends kept the largest of secrets from him. Anger flamed through him. Was there nobody left in this world he could trust? He clenched his hand around the glass tumbler until it threatened to shatter. "And you said nothing at all."

"I know it seems twisted, but we talked it through," he said, all humor gone, his smooth tones completely serious for once. "We thought this was the best way. You're too good at playing it cool with advance notice. You would have just made her mad."

"Like I didn't already do that?" He set aside the half-drunk glass of bourbon, the top-shelf brand wasted on him in his current mood.

"You confronted her with honesty," Malcolm answered reasonably. "If we'd given you time to think, you'd have gotten your pride up. You would have been angry and bullish. You can be rather pigheaded, you know."

"If I'm such a jackass, then why are we still friends?"

"Because I'm a jackass, too." Malcolm paused before continuing somberly. "You would have done the same for me. I know what it's like not to see your child, to have missed out on time you can never get back…"

Malcolm's voice choked off with emotion. He and his wife had been high school sweethearts who'd had to give up a baby girl for adoption since they were too young to provide a life for their daughter. Now they had twins—a boy and a girl—they loved dearly, but they still grieved for that first child, even knowing they'd made the right decision for her.

Although Malcolm and Celia had both known about *their* child from the start.

Elliot forked his hands through his buzzed hair, kept closely shorn since he'd let his thoughts of Lucy Ann distract him and he'd caught his car on fire just before Christmas—nearly caught himself on fire, as well.

He'd scorched his hair; the call had been that damn close.

"I just can't wrap my brain around the fact she's kept his existence from me for so long."

Malcolm snorted. "I can't believe the two of you slept together."

A growl rumbled low in his throat. "You're close to overstepping the bounds of our friendship with talk like that."

"Ahhh." He chuckled. "So you do care about her more than you've let on."

"We were...friends. Lifelong friends. That's no secret." He and Lucy Ann shared so much history it was impossible to unravel events from the past without thinking about each other. "The fact that there was briefly more...I can't deny that, either."

"You must not have been up to snuff for her to run so fast."

Anger hissed between Elliot's teeth, and he resisted the urge to pitch his Bluetooth over the balcony. "Now you have crossed the line. If we were sitting in the same place right now, my fist would be in your face."

"Fair enough." Douglas laughed softly again. "Like I said. You do care more than a little, more than any 'buddy.' And you can't refute it. Admit it, Elliot. I've just played you, my friend."

No use denying he'd been outmaneuvered by someone who knew him too well.

And as for what Malcolm had said? That he cared for Lucy Ann? Cared? Yes. He had. And like every other time in his life he'd cared, things had gone south.

If he wanted to sort through this mess and create any kind of future with Eli and Lucy Ann, he had to think more and care less.

Three

Lucy Ann shaded her eyes against the rising sun. For the third time in twenty-four hours a limousine pulled up her dusty road, oak trees creating a canopy for the long driveway. The first time had occurred yesterday when Elliot had arrived, then when he'd left, and now, he was returning.

Her simple semihermit life working from home with her son was drawing to a close in another few minutes.

Aunt Carla cradled Eli in her arms. Carla never seemed to age, her hair a perpetual shade halfway between gray and brown. She refused to waste money to have it colored. Her arms were ropy and strong from years of carting around trays of pizzas and sodas. Her skin was prematurely wrinkled from too much hard work, time in the Carolina sun—and a perpetual smile.

She was a tough, good woman who'd been there for Lucy Ann all her life. Too bad Carla couldn't have been her mother. Heaven knows she'd prayed for that often enough.

Carla smiled down at little Eli, his fist curled around her finger. "I'm sure I'm going to miss you both. It's been a treat having a baby around again."

She'd never had a child of her own, but was renowned for opening her home to family members in need. She wasn't a problem-solver so much as a temporary oasis. Very temporary, as the limo drew closer down the half-mile driveway.

"You're sweet to make it sound like we haven't taken over your house." Lucy Ann tugged her roller bag through the door, *kerthunking* it over a bump, casting one last glance back at the tiny haven of Hummels and the saggy sofa.

"Sugar, you know I only wish I could've done more for you this time and when you were young." Carla swayed from side to side, wearing her standard high-waisted jeans and a seasonal shirt—a pink Easter bunny on today's tee.

"You've always been there for me." Lucy Ann sat on top of her luggage, her eyes on the nearing limo. "I don't take that for granted."

"I haven't always been there for you and we both know it," Carla answered, her eyes shadowed with memories they both didn't like to revisit.

"You did the best you could. I know that." Since Lucy Ann's mother had legal guardianship and child services wouldn't believe any of the claims of neglect, much less allegations of abuse by stepfathers, there wasn't anything Lucy Ann could do other than escape to Carla—or to Elliot.

Her mother and her last stepfather had died in a boating accident, so there was nothing to be gained from dwelling on the past. Her mom had no more power over her than Lucy Ann allowed her. "Truly, Carla, the past is best left there."

"Glad to know you feel that way. I hope you learned that from me." Carla tugged on Lucy Ann's low ponytail. "If you can forgive me, why can't you forgive Elliot?"

Good question. She slouched back with a sigh. "If I could answer that, then I guess my heart wouldn't be breaking in two right now."

Her aunt hauled her in for a one-armed hug while she cradled the baby in the other. "I would fix this for you if I could."

"Come with us," Lucy Ann blurted. "I've asked you before and I know all your reasons for saying no. You love your home and your life and weekly bingo. But will you change your mind this time?" She angled back, hoping. "Will you come with us? We're family."

"Ah, sweet niece." Carla shook her head. "This is your life, your second chance, your adventure. Be careful. Be smart. And remember you're a damn amazing woman. He would be a lucky man to win you back."

Just the thought… No. "That's not why I'm going with him." She took Eli from her aunt. "My trip is only about planning a future for my son, for figuring out a way to blend Elliot's life with my new life."

"You used to be a major part of his world."

"I was his glorified secretary." A way for him to give her money while salving her conscience. At least she'd lived frugally and used the time to earn a degree so she could be self-sufficient. The stretch limo slowed along the last patch of gravel in front of the house.

"You were his best friend and confidant… And apparently something more at least once."

"I'm not sure what point you are trying to make, but

if you're going to make it, do so fast." She nodded to the opening limo door. "We're out of time."

"You two got along fabulously for decades and there's an obvious attraction. Why can't you have more?" Her aunt tipped her head, eyeing Elliot stepping from the vehicle. The car door slammed.

Sunshine sent dappled rays along his sandy-brown hair, over his honed body in casual jeans and a white polo that fit his muscled arms. She'd leaned on those broad shoulders for years without hesitation, but now all she could think about was the delicious feel of those arms around her. The flex of those muscles as he stretched over her.

Lucy Ann tore her eyes away and back to her aunt. "Have more?" That hadn't ended well for either of them. "Are you serious?"

"Why wouldn't I be?"

"He hasn't come looking for me for nearly a year. He let me go." Something that had hurt every day of the eleven months that passed. She waved toward him talking to his chauffeur. "He's only here now because his friends threw him on my doorstep."

"You're holding back because of your pride?" Her aunt tut-tutted. "You're throwing him and a possible future away because of pride?"

"Listen to me. *He* threw *me* away." She'd been an afterthought or nuisance to people her whole life. She wouldn't let her son live the same second-class existence. Panic began to set in. "Now that I think of it, I'm not sure why I even agreed to go with him—"

"Stop. Hold on." Carla grabbed her niece by the shoulders and steadied her. "Forget I said anything at all. Of course you have every reason to be upset. Go with him and figure out how to manage your son's future. And I'll always be here if you decide to return."

"If?" Lucy Ann rolled her eyes. "You mean when."

Carla pointed to the limo and the broad-shouldered man walking toward them. "Do you really think Elliot's going to want his son to grow up here?"

"Um, I mean, I hadn't thought…"

True panic set in as Lucy Ann realized she no longer had exclusive say over her baby's life. Of course Elliot would have different plans for his child. He'd spent his entire life planning how to get out of here, devising ways to build a fortune, and he'd succeeded.

Eli was a part of that now. And no matter how much she wanted to deny it, her life could never be simple again.

Elliot sprawled in the backseat of the limo while Lucy Ann adjusted the straps on Eli's infant seat, checking each buckle to ensure it fit with obvious seasoned practice. Her loose ponytail swung forward, the dome light bringing out the hints of honey in her light brown hair.

He dug his fingers into the butter-soft leather to keep from stroking the length of her hair, to see if it was as silky as he remembered. He needed to bide his time. He had her and the baby with him. That was a huge victory, especially after their stubborn year apart.

And now?

He had to figure out a way to make her stay. To go back to the way things were…except he knew things couldn't be exactly the same. Not after they'd slept together. Although he would have to tread warily there. He couldn't see her cheering over a "friends with benefits" arrangement. He'd have to take it a step at a time to gauge her mood. She needed to be reminded of all the history they shared, all the ways they got along so well.

She tucked a homemade quilt over Eli's tiny legs before shifting to sit beside him. Elliot knocked on the driver's window and the vehicle started forward on their journey to the airport.

"Lucy Ann, you didn't have to stay up late packing that suitcase." He looked at the discarded cashmere baby blanket she left folded to the side. "I told you I would take care of buying everything he needs."

His son would never ride a secondhand bike he'd unearthed at the junkyard. A sense of possessiveness stirred inside him. He'd ordered the best of the best for his child—from the car seat to a travel bed. Clothes. Toys. A stroller. He'd consulted his friends' wives for advice—easy enough since his buddies and their wives were all propagating like rabbits these days.

Apparently, so was he.

Lucy Ann rested a hand on the faded quilt with tiny blue sailboats. "Eli doesn't know if something is expensive or a bargain. He only knows if something feels or smells familiar. He's got enough change in his life right now."

"Is that a dig at me?" He studied her, trying to get a read on her mood. She seemed more reserved than yesterday, worried even.

"Not a dig at all. It's a fact." She eyed him with confusion.

"He has you as a constant."

"Damn straight he does," she said with a mama-bear ferocity that lit a fire inside him. Her strength, the light in her eyes, stirred him.

Then it hit him. She was in protective mode because she saw him as a threat. She actually thought he might try to take her child away from her. Nothing could be further from the truth. He wanted to parent the child *with* her.

He angled his head to capture her gaze fully. "I'm not trying to take him away from you. I just want to be a part of his life."

"Of course. That was always my intention," she said, her eyes still guarded, wary. "I know trust is difficult right now, but I hope you will believe me that I want you to have regular visitation."

Ah, already she was trying to set boundaries rather than thinking about possibilities. But he knew better than to fight with her. Finesse always worked better than head-on confrontation. He pointed to the elementary school they'd attended together, the same redbrick building but with a new playground. "We share a lot of history and now we share a son. Even a year apart isn't going to erase everything else."

"I understand that."

"Do you?" He moved closer to her.

Her body went rigid as she held herself still, keeping a couple of inches of space between them. "Remember when we were children, in kindergarten?"

Following her train of thought was tougher than maneuvering through race traffic, but at least she was talking to him. "Which particular day in kindergarten?"

She looked down at her hands twisted in her lap, her nails short and painted with a pretty orange. "You were lying belly flat on a skateboard racing down a hill."

That day eased to the front of his mind. "I fell off, flat on my ass." He winced. "Broke my arm."

"All the girls wanted to sign your cast." She looked sideways at him, smiling. "Even then you were a chick magnet."

"They just wanted to use their markers," he said dismissively.

She looked up to meet his eyes fully for the first time since they'd climbed into the limousine. "I knew that your arm was already broken."

"You never said a word to me." He rubbed his forearm absently.

"You would have been embarrassed if I confronted you, and you would have lied to me. We didn't talk as openly then about our home lives." She tucked the blanket more securely around the baby's feet as Eli sucked a pacifier in his sleep. "We were new friends who shared a jelly sandwich at lunch."

"We were new friends and yet you were right about the arm." He looked at his son's tiny hands and wondered how any father could ever strike out at such innocence. Sweat beaded his forehead at even the thought.

"I told my mom though, after school," Lucy Ann's eyes fell to his wrist. "She wasn't as…distant in those days."

The weight of her gaze was like a stroke along his skin, her words salve to a past wound. "I didn't know you said anything to anyone."

"Her word didn't carry much sway, or maybe she didn't fight that hard." She shrugged, the strap of her sundress sliding. "Either way, nothing happened. So I went to the principal."

"My spunky advocate." God, he'd missed her. And yet he'd always thought he knew everything about her and here she had something new to share. "Guess that explains why they pulled me out of class to interview me about my arm."

"You didn't tell the principal the truth though, did you?

I kept waiting for something big to happen. My five-year-old imagination was running wild."

For one instant in that meeting he had considered talking, but the thoughts of afterward had frozen any words in his throat like a lodged wad of that shared jelly sandwich. "I was still too scared of what would happen to my mother if I talked. Of what he would do to her."

Sympathy flickered in her brown eyes. "We discussed so many things as kids, always avoiding anything to do with our home lives. Our friendship was a haven for me then."

He'd felt the same. But that meeting with the principal had made him bolder later, except he'd chosen the wrong person to tell. Someone loyal to his father, which only brought on another beating.

"You had your secrets, too. I could always sense when you were holding back."

"Then apparently we didn't have any secrets from each other after all." She winced, her hand going to her son's car seat. "Not until this year."

The limo jostled along a pothole on the country road. Their legs brushed and his arm shot out to rest along the back of her seat. She jolted for an instant, her breath hitching. He stared back, keeping his arm in place until her shoulders relaxed.

"Oh, Elliot." She sagged back. "We're a mess, you and I, with screwed-up pasts and not much to go on as an example for building a future."

The worry coating her words stabbed at him. He cupped her arm lightly, the feel of her so damn right tucked to him. "We need to figure out how to straighten ourselves out to be good parents. For Eli."

"It won't be all that difficult to outdo our parents."

"Eli deserves a lot better than just a step above our

folks." The feel of her hair along his wrist soothed old wounds, the way she'd always done for him. But more than that, the feel of her now, with the new memories, with that night between them…

His pulse pounded in his ears, his body stirring…. He wanted her. And right now, he didn't see a reason why they couldn't have everything. They shared a similar past and they shared a child.

He just had to convince Lucy Ann. "I agree with you there. That's why it's important for us to use this time together wisely. Figure out how to be the parents he deserves. Figure out how to be a team, the partners he needs."

"I'm here, in the car with you, committed to spending the next four weeks with you." She tipped her face up to his, the jasmine scent of her swirling all around him. "What more do you want from me?"

"I want us to be friends again, Lucy Ann," he answered honestly, his voice raw. "Friends. Not just parents passing a kid back and forth to each other. I want things the way they were before between us."

Her pupils widened with emotion. "Exactly the way we were before? Is that even possible?"

"Not exactly as before," he conceded, easy enough to do when he knew his plans for something better between them.

He angled closer, stroking her ponytail over her shoulder in a sweep he wanted to take farther down her back to her waist. He burned all the way to his gut, needing to pull her closer.

"We'll be friends and more. We can go back to that night together, pick up from there. Because heaven help me, if we're being totally honest, then yes. I want you back in my bed again."

Four

The caress of Elliot's hand along her hair sent tingles all the way to her toes. She wanted to believe the deep desire was simply a result of nearly a year without sex, but she knew her body longed for this particular man. For the pleasure of his caress over her bare skin.

Except then she wouldn't be able to think straight. Now more than ever, she needed to keep a level head for her child. She loved her son more than life, and she had some serious fences to mend with Elliot to secure a peaceful future for Eli.

Lucy Ann clasped Elliot's wrist and moved it aside. "You can't be serious."

"I'm completely serious." His fingers twisted in her ponytail.

"Let. Go. Now," she said succinctly, barely able to keep herself from grabbing his shirt and hauling him in for a kiss. "Sex will only complicate matters."

"Or it could simplify things." He released her hair slowly, his stroke tantalizing all the way down her arm.

Biting her lip, she squeezed her eyes shut, too enticed by the green glow of desire in his eyes.

"Lucy Ann?" His bourbon-smooth tones intoxicated the parched senses that had missed him every day of the past eleven months. "What are you thinking?"

Her head angled ever so slightly toward his touch. "My aunt said the same thing about the bonus of friends becoming…more."

He laughed softly, the heat of his breath warming her throat and broadcasting just how close he'd moved to her, so close he could kiss the exposed flesh. "Your aunt has always been a smart woman. Although I sure as hell didn't talk to her about you and I becoming lovers."

She opened her eyes slowly, steeling herself. "You need to quit saying things like that or I'm going to have the car stopped right now. I will walk home with my baby if I have to. You and I need boundaries for this to work."

His gaze fell to her mouth for an instant that felt stretched to eternity before he angled back, leather seat creaking. "We'll have to agree to disagree."

Her exhale was shakier than she would have liked, betraying her. "You can cut the innocent act. I've seen your playboy moves over the years. Your practiced charm isn't going to work with me." Not again, anyway. "And it wouldn't have worked before if I hadn't been so taken away by sentimentality and a particularly strong vintage liqueur."

Furrows dug deep trenches in his forehead. "Lucy Ann, I am deeply sorry if I took advantage of our friendship—"

"I told you that night. No apologies." His apologies had been mortifying then, especially when she'd been hoping for a repeat only to learn he was full of regrets. He'd stung her pride and her heart. Not that she ever intended to let him know as much. "There were two of us in bed that night, and I refuse to call it a mistake. But it won't happen again, remember? We decided that then."

Or rather *he* had decided and *she* had pretended to go along to save face over her weakness when it came to this man.

His eyes went smoky. "I remember a lot of other things about that night."

Already she could feel herself weakening, wanting to read more into his every word and slightest action. She had to stop this intimacy, this romanticism, now.

"Enough talking about the past. This is about our future. Eli's future." She put on her best logical, personal-assistant voice she'd used a million times to place distance between them. "Where are we going first? I have to confess I haven't kept track of the race dates this year."

"Races later," he said simply as the car reached the airport. "First, we have a wedding to attend."

Her gut tightened at his surprise announcement. "A wedding?"

Lucy Ann hated weddings. Even when the wedding was for a longtime friend. Elliot's high school alumni pal—Dr. Rowan Boothe—was marrying none other than an African princess, who also happened to be a Ph.D. research scientist.

She hated to feel ungrateful, though, since this was the international event of the year, with a lavish ceremony in East Africa, steeped in colorful garb and local delicacies. Invitations were coveted, and media cameras hovered at a respectable distance, monitored by an elite security team that made the packed day run smoothly well into the evening. Tuxedos, formal gowns and traditional tribal wraps provided a magnificent blend of beauty that reflected the couple's modern tastes while acknowledging time-honored customs.

Sitting at the moonlit reception on the palace lawns by the beach, her baby asleep in a stroller, Lucy Ann sipped her glass of spiced fruit juice. She kept a smile plastered on her face as if her showing up here with Elliot and their son was nothing out of the ordinary. Regional music with drums and flutes carried on the air along with laughter and celebration. She refused to let her bad mood ruin the day for the happy bride and groom. Apparently, Elliot had been "kidnapped" from Rowan's bachelor party.

Now he'd returned for the wedding—with her and the baby. No one had asked, but their eyes all made it clear they knew. The fact that he'd thrust their messed-up relationship right into the spotlight frustrated her. But he'd insisted it was better to do it sooner rather than later. Why delay the inevitable?

He'd even arranged for formal dresses for her to pick from. She'd had no choice but to oblige him since her only formals were basic black, far too somber for a wedding. She'd gravitated toward simple wear in the past, never wanting to stand out. Although in this colorful event, her pale lavender gown wasn't too glaring. Still, she felt a little conspicuous because it was strapless and floor-length with a beaded bodice. Breast-feeding had given her new cleavage.

A fact that hadn't gone unnoticed, given the heated looks Elliot kept sliding her way.

But her mood was too sour to dwell on those steamy glances. Especially when he looked so mouth-wateringly handsome in a tuxedo, freshly shaven and smiling. It was as if the past eleven months apart didn't exist, as if they'd just shared the same bed, the same glass of wine. They'd been close friends for so long, peeling him from her thoughts was easier said than done.

She just wanted the marriage festivities to be over, then hopefully she would feel less vulnerable, more in control.

Weddings were happy occasions for some, evoking dreams or bringing back happy memories. Not for her. When she saw the white lace, flowers and a towering cake, she could only remember each time her mama said "I do." All four times. Each man was worse than the one before, until child services stepped in and said drug addict stepdaddy number four had to go if Lucy Ann's mother wanted to keep her child.

Mama chose hubby.

Lucy Ann finally went to live with her aunt for good— no more dodging groping hands or awkward requests to sit on "daddy's" lap. Her aunt loved her, cared for her, but Carla had others to care for, as well—Grandma and an older bachelor uncle.

No one put Lucy Ann first or loved her most. Not until this baby. She would do anything for Eli. Anything. Even swallow her pride and let Elliot back in her life.

Still, keeping on a happy face throughout the wedding was hard. All wedding phobia aside, she worked to appreciate the wedding as an event. She had to learn the art of detaching her emotions from her brain if she expected to make it through the next four weeks with her heart intact.

"Lucy Ann?" A familiar female voice startled her, and she set her juice aside to find Hillary Donavan standing beside her.

Hillary was married to another of Elliot's school friends, Troy Donavan, more commonly known as the

Robin Hood Hacker. As a computer-savvy teen he'd wreaked all sorts of havoc. Now he was a billionaire software developer. He'd recently married Hillary, an events planner, who looked as elegant as ever in a green Grecian-style silk dress.

The red-haired beauty dropped into a chair beside the stroller. "Do you mind if I hide out here with you and the baby for a while? My part in orchestrating this nationally televised wedding is done, thank heavens."

"You did a lovely job blending local traditions with a modern flair. No doubt magazine covers will be packed with photos."

"They didn't give me much time to plan since they made their engagement announcement just after Christmas, but I'm pleased with the results. I hope they are, too."

"I'm sure they are, although they can only see each other." Lucy Ann's stomach tightened, remembering her mother's adoring looks for each new man.

"To think they were professional adversaries for so long…now the sparks between them are so tangible I'm thinking I didn't need to order the firework display for a finale."

Lucy Ann pulled a tight smile, doing her best to be polite. "Romance is in the air."

"I hope this isn't going too late for you and the little guy." She flicked her red hair over her shoulder. "You must be exhausted from your flight."

"He's asleep. We'll be fine." If she left, Elliot would feel obligated to leave, as well. And right now she was too emotionally raw to be alone with him. Surely Hillary had to have some idea of how difficult this was for her, since the alum buddies had been party to the kidnapping.

Her eyes slid to the clutch of pals, the five men who'd been sent to a military reform school together.

Their bond was tight. Unbreakable.

They stood together at the beachside under a cabana wearing matching tuxedos, all five of them too damn rich and handsome for their own good. Luckily for the susceptible female population, the other four were now firmly taken, married and completely in love with their brides. The personification of bad boys redeemed, but still edgy. Exciting.

The Alpha Brotherhood rarely gathered in one place, but when they did, they were a sight to behold. They'd all landed in trouble with the law as teens, but they'd been sent to a military reform school rather than juvie. Computer whiz Troy Donavan had broken into the Department of Defense's computer system to expose corruption. Casino magnate Conrad Hughes had used insider trading tips to manipulate the stock market. He'd only barely redeemed himself by tanking corporations that used child-labor sweatshops in other countries. World famous soft rock/jazz musician Malcolm Douglas had been sent away on drug charges as a teenager, although she'd learned later that he'd been playing the piano in a bar underage and got nabbed in the bust.

The groom—Dr. Rowan Boothe—had a history a bit more troubled. He'd been convicted of driving while drunk. He'd been part of an accident he'd taken the blame for so his overage brother wouldn't go to jail—then his brother had died a year later driving drunk into a tree. Now Rowan used all his money to start clinics in third-world countries.

They all had their burdens to bear, and that guilt motivated them to make amends now. Through their freelance work with Interpol. Through charitable donations beyond anything anyone would believe unless they saw the accounting books.

Now, they'd all settled down and gotten married, starting families of their own. Was that a part of what compelled Elliot to push for more with her? A need to fit in with his Alpha Brothers as they moved on to the next phase of their lives?

Lucy Ann looked back at Hillary. "Did you know what Malcolm and Conrad were up to yesterday?"

"I didn't know exactly, not until Troy told me, and they were already on their way. I can't say I approve of their tactics, but it was too late for me to do anything. You appear to be okay." Hillary leaned on her elbows, angling closer, her eyes concerned. "Is that an act?"

"What do you think?"

She clasped Lucy Ann's hand. "I'm sorry. I should have realized this calm of yours is just a cover. We're kindred spirits, you and I, ever organized, even in how we show ourselves to the world." She squeezed once before letting go. "Do you want to talk? Need a shoulder? I'm here."

"There's nothing anyone can do now. It's up to Elliot and me to figure out how to move forward. If I'd let him know earlier…"

"Friend, you and I both know how difficult it can be to contact them when the colonel calls for one of their missions. They disappear. They're unreachable." She smiled sadly. "It takes something as earth-shattering as, well, a surprise baby to get them to break the code of silence."

"How do you live with that, as a part of a committed relationship?"

She couldn't bring herself to ask what it felt like to be married to a man who kept such a chunk of his life separate. She'd known as a friend and as a personal assistant that Elliot's old headmaster later recruited previous students as freelancers for Interpol. She'd kept thoughts about that segmented away, since it did not pertain to her job or their life on the race circuit.

But now, there was no denying that her life was tied to Elliot's in a much deeper way.

"I love Troy, the man he is. The man he's always been," Hillary said. "We grow, we mature, but our basic natures stay the same. And I love who that man is."

Lucy Ann could almost—almost—grasp the promise in that, except she knew Hillary helped her husband on some of those missions, doing a bit of freelance work of her own.

Lucy Ann stared down into the amber swirl of her juice glass. "Is it so wrong to want an ordinary life? I don't mean to sound ungrateful, but *normal,* boring, well, I've never had that. I crave it for myself and my child, but it feels so unattainable."

"That's a tough one, isn't it? These men are many things, but normal—delightfully boring—doesn't show up anywhere on that list."

Where did that leave her? In search of what she couldn't have? Or a hypocrite for not accepting Elliot the way he had accepted her all her life? She ran from him. As much as she swore that he pushed her away, she knew. She'd run just as fast and hard as he'd pushed.

"Thank you for the advice, Hillary."

Her friend sighed. "I'm not sure how much help I've been. But if you need to talk more, I'm here for you. I won't betray your confidences."

"I appreciate that," Lucy Ann said, and meant it, only just realizing how few female friends she'd ever had. Elliot had been her best friend and she'd allowed that to close her off to other avenues of support.

"Good, very good. We women need to stick together, make a sisterhood pact of our own." She winked before ducking toward the stroller. "Little Eli is adorable, and I'm glad you're here."

Lucy Ann appreciated the gesture, and she wanted to trust. She wanted to believe there could be a sisterhood of support in dealing with these men—even though she wouldn't be married to Elliot. Still, their lives were entwined because of their child.

A part of her still wondered, doubted. The wives of Elliot's friends had reached out initially after she left, but eventually they'd stopped. Could she really be a part of their sisterhood?

"Thank you, Hillary," she said simply, her eyes sliding back to Elliot standing with his friends.

Her hand moved protectively over to the handle of her son's stroller, her throat constricting as she took in the gleaming good looks of her baby's father. Even his laugh seemed to make the stars shimmer brighter.

And how frivolous a thought was that?

She definitely needed to keep her head on straight and her heart locked away. She refused to be anyone's obligation or burden ever again.

Elliot hoped Rowan and Mariama's marriage ceremony would soften Lucy Ann's mood. After all, weren't weddings supposed to make women sentimental? He'd watched her chatting with his friends' wives and tried to gauge her reaction. She knew them all from her time working as his assistant, and seeing this big extended family connected by friendship rather than blood should appeal to her. They'd talked about leaving their pasts behind countless times as kids.

They could fit right in here with their son. A practical decision. A fun life.

So why wasn't she smiling as the bride and groom drove away in a BMW convertible, the bride's veil trailing in the wind?

Shouldering free of the crowd, Elliot made his way toward Lucy Ann, who stood on the periphery, their son in a stroller beside her. Even though he'd arranged for a nanny who'd once worked for a British duke, Lucy Ann said she couldn't let her son stay with a total stranger. She would need to conduct her own interview tomorrow. If the woman met her standards, she could help during Eli's naps so Lucy Ann could keep up with the work obligations she hadn't been able to put on hold. The encounter still made Elliot grin when he thought of her refusing to be intimidated by the very determined Mary Poppins.

He stopped beside Lucy Ann, enjoying the way the moonlight caressed her bare shoulders. Her hair was loose and lifting in the night wind. Every breath he took drew in hints of her, of Carolina jasmine. His body throbbed to life with a reminder of what they could have together, something so damn amazing he'd spent eleven months running from the power of it.

Now, fate had landed him here with her. Running wasn't an option, and he found that for once he didn't mind fate kicking him in the ass.

Elliot rested his hand on the stroller beside hers, watching every nuance of her reaction. "Are you ready to call it a day and return to our suite, or would you like to take a walk?"

She licked her lips nervously. "Um, I think a walk, perhaps."

So she wasn't ready to be alone with him just yet? A promising sign, actually; she wanted him still, even if she wasn't ready to act on that desire. Fine, then. He could use the moon and stars to romance her, the music from a steel drum band serenading them.

"A walk it is, then, Lucy dear," he asserted.

"Where can we go with a baby?"

He glanced around at the party with guests still dancing along the cabana-filled beach. Tables of food were still laden with half shares of delicacies, fruits and meats. A fountain spewing wine echoed the rush of waves along the shore. Mansions dotted the rocky seashore, with a planked path leading to docks.

"This way." He gestured toward the shoreline board-walk, all but deserted this late at night. "I'll push the stroller."

He stepped behind the baby carriage. Lucy Ann had no choice but to step aside or they would be stuck hip to hip, step for step.

Five minutes later, they'd left the remnants of the reception behind, the stroller wheels rumbling softly along the wooden walkway. To anyone looking from the looming mansions above, lights shining from the windows like eyes, he and Lucy Ann would appear a happy family walking with their son.

Tonight more than ever he was aware of his single status. Yet again, he'd stood to the side as another friend got married. Leaving only him as a bachelor. But he was a father now. There was no more running from fears of becoming his father. He had to be a man worthy of this child. His child with Lucy Ann.

She walked beside him, the sea breeze brushing her gauzy dress along his leg in phantom caresses. "You're quite good at managing that stroller. I'm surprised. It took me longer than I expected to get the knack of not knocking over everything in my path."

He smiled at her, stuffing down a spark of anger along with the urge to remind her that he would have helped in those early days if she'd only let him know. "It's just like maneuvering a race car."

"Of course. That makes sense."

"More sense than me being at ease with a child? I'm determined to get this right, Lucy Ann, don't doubt that for a second." Steely determination fueled his words.

"You used to say you never wanted kids of your own."

Could those words have made her wary of telling him? There had been a time when they shared everything with each other.

He reminded her, "You always insisted that you didn't want children, either."

"I didn't want to risk putting any child in my mother's path." She rubbed her hand along her collarbone, the one she'd cracked as a child. "I'm an adult now and my mother's passed away. But we're talking about *you* and your insistence that you didn't want kids."

"I didn't. Then." If things hadn't changed, he still might have said the same, but one look in Eli's wide brown eyes and his world had altered in an instant. "I don't run away from responsibilities."

"You ran away before—" She stopped short, cursing softly. "Forget I said that."

Halting, he pulled his hands from the stroller, the baby sleeping and the carriage tucked protectively between them and the railing.

Elliot took her by the shoulders. Her soft bare shoulders. So vulnerable. So...*her*. "Say it outright, Lucy Ann. I left *you* behind when I left Columbia behind, when I let myself get sloppy and caught, when I risked jail because anything seemed better than staying with my father. For a selfish instant, I forgot about what that would mean for you. And I've regretted that every day of my life."

The admission was ripped from his throat; deeper still, torn all the way from his gut. Except there was no one but Lucy Ann to hear him on the deserted walkway. Stone houses dotted the bluff, quarters for guests and staff, all structures up on the bluff with a few lights winking in the night. Most people still partied on at the reception.

"I understand that you feel guilty. Like you have to make up for things. But you need to stop thinking that way. I'm responsible for my own life." She cupped his face, her eyes softening. "Besides, if you'd stayed, you wouldn't have this amazing career that also gave me a chance to break free. So I guess it all worked out in the end."

"Yet you ended up returning home when you left me." Hell, he should be honest now while he had the chance. He didn't want to waste an instant or risk the baby waking up and interrupting them. "When I stupidly pushed you away."

Her arm dropped away again. "I returned with a degree and the ability to support myself and my child. That's significant and I appreciate it." Her hands fisted at her sides. "I don't want to be your obligation."

"You want a life of your own, other than being my assistant. I understand that." He kept his voice low, which brought her closer to listen over the crash of waves below the boardwalk. He liked having her close again. "Let's talk it through, like we would have in the old days."

"You're being so—" she scowled "—so reasonable."

"You say that like it's a dirty word. Why is that a bad thing?" Because God help him, he was feeling anything but reasonable. If she wanted passion and emotion, he was more than willing to pour all of that into seducing her. He just had to be sure before he made a move.

A wrong step could set back his cause.

"Don't try to manipulate me with all the logical reasons why I should stay. I want you to be honest about what you're thinking. What you *want* for your future."

"When it comes to the future, I don't know what I want, Lucy Ann, beyond making sure you and Eli are safe, provided for, never afraid. I'm flying by the seat of my pants here, trying my best to figure out how to get through this being-a-father thing." Honesty was ripping a hole in him. He wanted to go back to logic.

Or passion.

Her chest rose and fell faster with emotion, a flush spreading across her skin in the moon's glow. "How would things have been different if I had come to you, back when I found out I was pregnant?"

"I would have proposed right away," he said without hesitation.

"I would have said no," she answered just as quickly.

He stepped closer. "I would have been persistent in trying to wear you down."

"How would you have managed that?"

The wind tore at her dress, whipping the skirt forward to tangle in his legs, all but binding them together with silken bands.

He angled his face closer to hers, his mouth so close he could claim her if he moved even a whisker closer. "I would have tried to romance you with flowers, candy and jewels." He watched the way her pupils widened with awareness as his words heated her cheek. "Then I would have realized you're unconventional and I would have changed tactics."

"Such as?" she whispered, the scent of fruit juice on her breath, dampening her lips. "Be honest."

"Hell, Lucy Ann, if you want honesty, here it is." His hand slid up her bare arm, along her shoulder, under her hair, to cup the back of her neck, and God, it felt good to touch her after so long apart. It felt right. "I just want to kiss you again."

Five

Lucy Ann gripped Elliot's shoulders, her fingers digging in deep by instinct even as her brain shouted "bad idea."

Her body melted into his, the hard planes of his muscular chest absorbing the curves of her, her breasts hypersensitive to the feel of him. And his hands... A sigh floated from her into him. His hands were gentle and warm and sure along her neck and into her hair, massaging her scalp. Her knees went weak, and he slid an arm down to band around her waist, securing her to him.

How could he crumble her defenses with just one touch of his mouth to hers? But she couldn't deny it. A moonlight stroll, a starlight kiss along the shore had her dreaming romantic notions. Made her want more.

Want him.

His tongue stroked along the seam of her mouth, and she opened without hesitation, taking him every bit as much as he took her. Stroking and tasting. There was a certain safety in the moment, out here in the open, since there was no way things could go further. Distant guest houses, the echoes of the reception carrying on the wind and of course the baby with them kept her from being totally swept away.

Her hands glided down his sides to tuck into his back pockets, to cup the taut muscles that she'd admired on more than one occasion. Hell, the whole female population had admired that butt thanks to a modeling gig he'd taken early in his career to help fund his racing. She'd ribbed him about those underwear ads, even knowing he was blindingly hot. She'd deluded herself into believing she was objective, immune to his sensuality, which went beyond mere good looks.

The man had a rugged charisma that oozed machismo.

Heaven help her, she wanted to dive right in and swim around, luxuriating in the sensations. The tingling in her breasts sparked through her, gathering lower with a familiar intensity she recognized too well after their night together.

This had to stop. Now. Because mistakes she'd made this time wouldn't just hurt her—or Elliot. They had a child to consider. A precious innocent life only a hand's reach away.

With more than a little regret, she ended the kiss, nipping his sensuous bottom lip one last time. His growl of frustration rumbled his chest against hers, but he didn't stop her. Her head fell to rest on his shoulder as she inhaled the scent of sea air tinged with the musk of his sweat. As Elliot cupped the back of her head in a broad palm, his ragged breaths reassured her he was every bit as affected by the kiss. An exciting and yet dangerous reality that confused her after the way they'd parted a year ago.

She needed space to think through this. Maybe watching the wedding and seeing all those happy couples had affected her more than she realized. Even just standing here in his arms with the feel of his arousal pressing against her stomach, she was in serious danger of making a bad choice if she stayed with him a moment longer.

Flattening her palms to his chest, Lucy Ann pushed, praying her legs would hold when he backed away.

She swayed for an instant before steeling her spine. "Elliot, this—" she gestured between them, then touched her kissed tender lips softly "—this wasn't part of our bargain when we left South Carolina. Or was it?"

The night breeze felt cooler now, the sea air chilly.

His eyes stayed inscrutable as he stuffed his hands in his tuxedo pockets, the harsh planes of his face shadowed by moonlight. "Are you accusing me of plotting a seduction?"

"*Plotting* is a harsh word," she conceded, her eyes flitting to the baby in his stroller as she scrambled to regain control of her thoughts, "but I think you're not above planning to do whatever it takes to get your way. That's who you are. Can you deny it?"

His eyes glinted with determination—and anger? "I won't deny wanting to sleep with you. The way you kissed me back gives me the impression you're on board with that notion."

Her heartbeat quickened with visions of how easy it would be to fall into bed with him. To pick up where they'd left off a year ago. If only she had any sense he wanted her for more than a connection to his son.

"That's the point, Elliot. It doesn't matter what *we* want. This month together is supposed to be about building a future for *Eli*. More of—" she gestured between them, her heart tripping over itself at just the mention of their kiss, their attraction "—playing with fire only risks an unstable future for our son. We need to recapture our friendship. Nothing more."

Her limbs felt weak at even the mention of *more*.

He arched an arrogant eyebrow. "I disagree that they're mutually exclusive."

"If you push me on this, I'll have to leave the tour and return to South Carolina." She'd seen too often how easily he seduced women. He was a charmer, without question, and she refused to be like her mother, swept away into reckless relationships again and again. She had a level head and she needed to keep it. "Elliot, do you hear me? I need to know we're on the same page about these next four weeks."

He studied her through narrowed eyes for the crash of four rolling waves before he shrugged. "I will respect your wishes, and I will keep my hands to myself." He smiled, pulling his hands from his pockets and holding them up. "Unless you change your mind, of course."

"I won't," she said quickly, almost too forcefully for her own peace of mind. That old Shakespeare quote came back to her, taunting her, *Methinks the lady doth protest too much.*

"Whoa, whoa, hold on now." Elliot patted the air. "I'm not trying to make you dig in your stubborn heels, so let's end this conversation and call it a day. We can talk more tomorrow, in the light of day."

"Less ambiance would be wise." Except she knew he looked hunky in any light, any situation.

Regardless of how much she wanted to go back, she realized that wasn't possible. They'd crossed a line the night they went too far celebrating his win and her completing her final exams.

It had never happened before she had a plan for her

own future. The catalyst had been completing her degree, feeling that for the first time since they were kids, she met him on an even footing. She'd allowed her walls to come down. She'd allowed herself to acknowledge what she'd been hiding all her adult life. She was every bit as attracted to Elliot Starc as his fawning groupies.

What if she was no different from her mother?

The thought alone had her staggering for steady ground. She grabbed the stroller just to be on the safe side. "I'm going back to the room now. It's time to settle Eli for the night. I need to catch up on some work before I go to sleep. And I do mean sleep."

"Understood," he said simply from beside her. "I'll walk back with you."

The heat of him reached her even though their bodies didn't touch. Just occupying the same space as him offered a hefty temptation right now.

She shook her head, the glide of her hair along her bared shoulders teasing her oversensitized skin. "I'd rather go alone. The palace is in sight and the area's safe."

"As you wish." He stepped back with a nod and a half bow. "We'll talk tomorrow on the way to Spain." He said it as a promise, not a request.

"Okay then," she conceded softly over her shoulder as she pushed the stroller, wheeling it toward the palace where they were staying in one of the many guest suites. Her body still hummed from the kiss, but her mind filled with questions and reservations.

She and Elliot had been platonic friends for years, comfortable with each other. As kids, they'd gone skinny-dipping, built forts in the woods, comforted each other during countless crises and disappointments. He'd been her best friend…right up to the moment he wasn't. Where had this crazy attraction between them come from?

The wheels of the stroller whirred along the walkway as fast as the memories spinning through her. That night eleven months ago when they'd been together had been spontaneous but amazing. She'd wondered if maybe there could be more between them. The whole friends-with-benefits had sounded appealing, taking it a day at a time until they sorted out the bombshell that had been dropped into their relationship: a sexual chemistry that still boggled her mind.

And yet Elliot's reaction the next day had made her realize there could be no future for them. Her euphoria had evaporated with the morning light.

She'd woken before him and gone to the kitchen to make coffee and pile some pastries on a plate. The front door to his suite had opened and she'd assumed it must be the maid. Anyone who entered the room had to have a key and a security code.

However, the woman who'd walked in hadn't been wearing a uniform. She—Gianna—had worn a trench coat and nothing else. If only it had been a crazed fan. But Lucy Ann had quickly deduced Gianna was the new female in Elliot's life. He hadn't even denied it. There was no misunderstanding.

God, it had been so damn cliché her stomach had roiled. Elliot came out of the bedroom and Gianna had turned paler than the towel around Elliot's waist.

He'd kept his calm. Apologized to Gianna for the awkward situation, but she'd burst into tears and run. He'd told Lucy Ann there was nothing between him and his girlfriend anymore, not after what happened the night before with Lucy Ann.

But she'd told him he should have let Gianna know that first, and she was a hundred percent right. He'd agreed and apologized.

That hadn't been enough for her. The fact that he could be seeing one woman, even superficially, and go to bed with another? No, no and hell, no. That was something she couldn't forgive. Not after how all those men had cheated on her mom with little regard for vows or promises. And her mother kept forgiving the first unfaithful jerk, and then the next.

If Elliot could behave this way now, how could she trust him later? What if he got "swept away" by someone else and figured he would clue her in later? She'd called him dishonorable.

And in an instant, with that one word, a lifetime friendship crumbled.

She'd thrown on her clothes and left. Elliot's engagement to Gianna a month later had only sealed Lucy Ann's resolve to stay away. They hadn't spoken again until the day he'd shown up in Carla's yard.

Now, after more impulsive kisses, she found herself wanting to crawl right back into bed with him. Lucy Ann powered the stroller closer to the party and their quarters, drawing in one deep breath of salty air after another, willing her pulse to steady. Wishing the urge to be with Elliot was as easily controlled.

With each step, she continued the chant in her brain, the vow not to repeat her mother's mistakes.

Wind tearing at his tuxedo jacket, Elliot watched Lucy Ann push the stroller down the planked walkway, then past the party. He didn't take his eyes off her or his son until he saw they'd safely reached the palace, even though he now had bodyguards watching his family 24/7. His family?

Hell, yes, his family.

Eli was his son. And Lucy Ann had been his only real

family for most of his life. No matter how angry he got at her for holding back on telling him about Eli, Elliot also couldn't forgive himself for staying away from her. He'd let her down in a major way more than once, from his teenage years up to now. She had reason not to trust him.

He needed to earn back her trust. He owed her that and so much more.

His shoulders heaving with a sigh, he started toward the wedding reception. The bride and groom had left, but the partying would go long into the night. It wasn't every day a princess got married. People would expect a celebration to end all celebrations.

A sole person peeled away from the festivities and ambled toward him. From the signature streamlined fedora, he recognized his old school pal Troy Donavan. Troy was one of the originals from their high school band, the Alpha Brotherhood, a group of misfits who found kindred spirits in one another and their need to push boundaries, to expose hypocrisy—the greatest of crimes in their eyes.

Troy pulled up alongside him, passing him a drink. "Reconciliation not going too well?"

"What makes you say that?" He took the thick cut glass filled with a locally brewed beer.

"She's returning to her room alone after a wedding." Troy tipped his glass as if in a toast toward the guests. "More people get lucky after weddings than any other event known to mankind. That's why you brought Lucy Ann here, isn't it? To get her in the romantic mood."

Had he? He'd told himself he wanted her to see his friends settling down. For her to understand he could do the same. But he wasn't sure how much he felt like sharing, especially when his thoughts were still jumbled.

"I brought Lucy Ann to the wedding because I couldn't

miss the event. The timing has more to do with how you all colluded to pull off that kidnapping stunt."

"You're still pissed off? Sorry, dude, truly," he said, wincing. "I thought you and Malcolm talked that all out."

"Blah, blah, blah, my good pals wanted to get an unguarded reaction. I heard." And it still didn't sit well. He'd trusted these guys since high school, over fifteen years, and hell, yeah, he felt like they'd let him down. "But I also heard that Lucy Ann contacted the Brotherhood over a week ago. That's a week I lost with my son. A week she was alone caring for him. Would you be okay with that?"

"Fair enough. You have reason to be angry with us." Troy nudged his fedora back on his head. "But don't forget to take some of the blame yourself. She was your friend all your life, and you just let her go. You're going to have a tough as hell time convincing her you've magically changed your mind now and you would have wanted her back even without the kid."

The truth pinched. "Tell me something I don't know."

"Okay then. Here's a bit of advice."

"Everyone seems full of it," Elliot responded, tongue in cheek.

Troy laughed softly, leaning back against a wrought-iron railing. "Fine. I'm full of it. Always have been. Now, on to my two cents."

"By all means." Elliot knocked back another swallow of the local beer.

"You're a father now." Troy rolled his glass between his palms. "Be that boy's father and let everything else fall into place."

A sigh rattled through Elliot. "You make it sound so simple."

Troy's smile faded, no joking in sight. "Think how different our lives would have been with different parents.

Things came together when Salvatore gave us direction. Be there for your son."

"Relationships aren't saved by having a child together." His parents had gotten married because he was on the way. His mother had eventually walked out and left him behind.

"True enough. But they sure as hell are broken up by fighting over the child. Be smart in how you work together when it comes to Eli and it might go a long way toward smoothing things out with Lucy Ann." Troy ran a finger along the collar of his tuxedo shirt, edging a little more air for himself around his tie. "If not, you've got a solid relationship with your kid, and that's the most important thing."

Was his focus all wrong by trying to make things right with Lucy Ann? Elliot had to admit Troy's plan made some sense. The stakes were too important to risk screwing up with his son. "When did you get to be such a relationship sage?"

"Hillary's a smart woman, and I'm smart enough to listen to her." His sober expression held only for a second longer before he returned to the more lighthearted Troy they were all accustomed to. "Now more than ever I need to listen to Hillary's needs since she's pregnant."

"Congratulations to you both." Elliot clapped Troy on the back, glad for his friend even as he wondered what it might have been like to be by Lucy Ann's side while she was expecting Eli. "Who'd have predicted all this home and hearth for us a few years ago?"

"Colonel Salvatore's going to have to find some new recruits."

"You're not pulling Interpol missions?" That surprised him. Elliot understood Hillary's stepping out of fieldwork while pregnant. But he wouldn't have thought Troy would ever back off the edge.

"There are other ways I can help with my tech work. Who knows, maybe I'll even take on the mentorship role like Salvatore someday. But I'm off the clock now and missing my wife." Troy walked backward, waving once before he sprinted toward the party.

Elliot knew his friend was right. The advice made sense. Focus on the baby. But that didn't stop him from wanting Lucy Ann in his bed again. The notion of just letting everything fall into place was completely alien to his nature. He'd never been the laid-back sort like Troy. Elliot needed to move, act, win.

He needed Lucy Ann back in his life.

For months he'd told himself the power of Lucy Ann's kiss, of the sex they'd shared nearly a year ago, had been a hazy memory distorted by alcohol. But now, with his body still throbbing from the kiss they'd just shared, his hair still mussed, the memory of their hands running frenetically—hungrily—over each other, he knew. Booze had nothing to do with the explosive chemistry between them. Although Gianna's arrival had sure as hell provided a splash of ice water on the morning-after moment.

He'd screwed up by not breaking things off with Gianna before he let anything happen between him and Lucy Ann. He still wasn't sure why he and Gianna had reconciled afterward. He hadn't been fair to either woman. The dishonor in that weighed on him every damn day.

At least he'd finally done right by Gianna when they'd broken up. Now, he had to make things right with Lucy Ann.

Their kiss ten minutes ago couldn't lead to anything more, not tonight. He accepted that. It was still too early in his campaign to win her over. But a kiss? He could have that much for now at least. A taste of her, a hint of what more they could have together.

A hint of Lucy Ann was so much more than everything with any other woman.

She was so much a part of his life. Why the hell had he let her go?

This didn't have to be complicated. Friendship. Sex. Travel the world and live an exciting life together. He had a fortune at his disposal. They could stay anywhere, hire teachers to travel with them. Eli would have the best of everything and an education gleaned from seeing the world rather than just reading about it. Surely Lucy Ann would see that positively.

How could she say no to a future so much more secure than what they'd grown up with? He'd been an idiot not to press his case with her last time. But when she'd left before, he'd thought to give her space. This time, he would be more persistent.

Besides, last time he'd been a jerk and tried to goad her into returning by making the news with moving on—a total jackass decision he never would have made if he'd thought for a second that Lucy Ann might be pregnant.

Now, he would be wiser. Smoother.

He would win her over. They'd been partners before. They could be partners again.

Lucy Ann peered out the window of the private jet as they left Africa behind.

Time for their real journey to begin. It had been challenging enough being together with his friends, celebrating the kind of happily ever after that wasn't in the cards for her. But now came the bigger challenge—finding a way to parent while Elliot competed in the Formula One circuit. A different country every week—Spain, Monaco, Canada, England. Parties and revelry and yes, decadence, too. She felt guilty for enjoying it all, but she couldn't deny that she'd missed the travel, experiencing different cultures without a concern for cost. Plus, his close-knit group of friends gave them a band of companionship no matter what corner of the earth he traveled to during racing season.

She sank deeper into the luxury of the leather sofa, the sleek chrome-and-white interior familiar from their countless trips in the past, with one tremendous exception. Their son was secured into his car seat beside her, sleeping in his new race car pj's with a lamb's wool blanket draped over his legs. She touched his impossibly soft cheek, stroking his chubby features with a soothing hand, cupping his head, the dusting of blond hair so like his father's.

Her eyes skated to Elliot standing in the open bulkhead, talking to the pilot. Her former best friend and boss grew hotter with each year that passed—not fair. That didn't stop her from taking in the sight of him in low-slung jeans and a black button-down shirt with the sleeves rolled up. Italian leather loafers. He looked every bit the world-famous race car driver and heartthrob.

How long would Elliot's resolution to build a family life for Eli last? Maybe that's what this trip was about. Proving to *him* it couldn't be done. She wouldn't keep his son from him, but she refused to expose her child to a chaotic life. Eli needed and deserved stability.

And what did she want?

She pressed a hand to her stomach, her belly full of butterflies that had nothing to do with a jolt of turbulence. Just the thought of kissing Elliot last night... She dug her fingers into the supple leather sofa to keep from reaching for him as he walked toward her.

"Would you like something to eat or drink?" he asked, pausing by the kitchenette. "Or something to read?"

She knew from prior trips that he kept a well-stocked library of the classics as well as the latest bestsellers loaded on ereaders for himself and fellow travelers. In school, he'd always won the class contest for most books read in a year. He told her once those stories offered him an escape from his day-to-day life.

"No, thank you. The brunch before we left was amazing."

True enough, although she hadn't actually eaten much. She'd been so caught up in replaying the night before. In watching his friends' happy marriages with their children and babies on the way until her heart ached from all she wanted for her son.

For herself, as well.

Elliot slid onto the sofa beside her, leaning over her to adjust the blanket covering Eli's legs. "Tell me about his routine."

She sat upright, not expecting that question at all. "You want to know about Eli's schedule? Why?"

"He's my son." His throat moved with a long swallow of emotion at the simple sentence. "I should know what he needs."

"He has a mom, and he even has a nanny now." The British nanny was currently in the sleeping quarters reading or napping or whatever nannies did when they realized mothers needed a breather from having them around all the time.

Elliot tapped Lucy Ann's chin until she looked at him again. "And he has a dad."

"Of course," she agreed, knowing it was best for Eli,

but unused to sharing him. "If you're asking for diaper duty, you're more than welcome to it."

Would he realize her halfhearted attempt at a joke was meant to ease this tenacious tension between them? They used to be so in tune with each other.

"Diaper duty? Um, I was thinking about feeding and naps, that kind of thing."

"He breastfeeds," she said bluntly.

His eyes fell to her chest. The stroke of his gaze made her body hum as tangibly as the airplane engines.

Elliot finally cleared his throat and said, "Well, that could be problematic for me. But I can bring him to you. I can burp him afterward. He still needs to be burped, right?"

"Unless you want to be covered in baby spit-up." She crossed her arms over her chest.

He pulled his eyes up to her face. "Does he bottle-feed, too? If so, I can help out that way."

Fine, he wanted to play this game, then she would meet him point for point. "You genuinely think you can wake up during the night and then race the next day?"

"If you can function on minimal sleep, then so can I. You need to accept that we're in this together now."

He sounded serious. But then other than his playboy ways, he was a good man. A good friend. A philanthropist who chose to stay anonymous with his donations. She knew about them only through her work as his assistant.

"That's why I agreed to come with you, for Eli and in honor of our friendship in the past."

"Good, good. I'm glad you haven't forgotten those years. That friendship is something we can build on. But I'm not going to deny the attraction, Lucy Ann." He slid his arm along the back of the sofa seat, stretching his legs out in front of him. "I can't. You've always been pretty, but you looked incredible last night. Motherhood suits you."

"Flattery?" She picked up his arm and moved it to his lap. "Like flowers and candy? An obvious arm along the back? Surely you've got better moves than that."

"Are you saying compliments are wasted on you?" He picked up a lock of her hair, teasing it between two fingers. "What if I'm telling the truth about how beautiful you are and how much I want to touch you?"

She rolled her eyes, even though she could swear electricity crackled up the strand of hair he held. "I've watched your moves on women for years, remember?"

"It's not a move." He released the lock and smoothed it into the rest before crossing his arms. "If I were planning a calculated seduction for you, I would have catered a dinner, with a violin."

She crinkled her nose. "A violin? Really?"

"No privacy. Right." His emerald eyes studied her, the wheels in his brain clearly churning. "Maybe I would kiss you on the cheek, distract you by nuzzling your ear while tucking concert tickets into your pocket."

"Concert tickets?" She lifted an eyebrow with interest. They'd gone to free concerts in the park when they were teenagers.

"We would fly out to a show in another country, France or Japan perhaps."

She shook her head. "You're going way overboard. Too obvious. Rein it in, be personal."

"Flowers…" He snapped his fingers. "No wait. A single flower, something different, like a sprig of jasmine because the scent reminds me of you."

That silenced her for a moment. "You know my perfume?"

He dipped his head toward her ever so slightly as if

catching a whiff of her fragrance even now. "I know you smell like home in all the good ways. And I have some very good memories of home. They all include you."

Damn him, he was getting to her. His words affected her but she refused to let him see that. She schooled her features, smiling slightly. "Your moves have improved."

"I'm only speaking the truth." His words rang with honesty, his eyes heated with attraction.

"I do appreciate that about you, how we used to be able to tell each other anything." Their friendship had given her more than support. He'd given her hope that they could leave their pasts behind in a cloud of dust. "If we can agree to be honest now, that will work best."

"And no more secrets."

She could swear a whisper of hurt smoked through his eyes.

Guilt stabbed through her all over again. She owed him and there was no escaping that. "I truly am sorry I held back about Eli. That was wrong of me. Can you forgive me?"

"I have to, don't I?"

"No." She swallowed hard. "You don't."

"If I want us to be at peace—" he reached out and took her hand, the calluses on his fingertips a sweet abrasion along her skin "—then yes, I do."

She wasn't sure how that honest answer settled within her because it implied he wasn't really okay with what she'd done. He was only moving past it out of necessity. The way he'd shrugged off all the wrongs his father had done because he had no choice.

Guilt hammered her harder with every heartbeat, and she didn't have a clue how to make this right with him. She had as little practice with forgiveness and restitution as he did.

So she simply said, "Peace is a very good thing."

"Peace doesn't have to be bland." His thumb stroked the inside of her wrist.

Her pulse kicked up under his gentle stroking. "I didn't say that."

"Your tone totally implied it. You all but said 'boring.'" His shoulder brushed hers as he settled in closer, seducing her with his words, his husky tones every bit as much as his touch. "A truce can give freedom for all sorts of things we never considered before."

"News flash, Elliot. The kissing part. We've considered that before."

"Nice." He clasped her wrist. "You're injecting some of your spunky nature into the peace. That's good. Exciting. As brilliantly shiny as your hair with those new streaks of honey added by the Carolina sun."

Ah, now she knew why he'd been playing with her hair. "Added by my hairdresser."

"Liar."

"How do you know?"

"Because I'm willing to bet you've been squirrelling away every penny you make. I can read you—most of the time." He skimmed his hand up her arm to stroke her hair back over her shoulder. "While I know that you want me, I can't gauge what you intend to do about that, because make no mistake, I want us to pursue that. I said before that motherhood agrees with you and I meant it. You drove me crazy last night in that evening gown."

He continued to stroke her arm, but she couldn't help but think if she moved even a little, his hand would brush her breast. Even the phantom notion of that touch had her tingling with need.

She worked to keep her voice dry—and to keep from grabbing him by the shirtfront and hauling him toward her. "You're taking charming to a new level. I'm impressed."

"Good. But are you seduced?"

"You're good, and I'm enticed," she said, figuring she might as well be honest. No use denying the obvious. "But Elliot, this isn't a fairy tale. Our future is not going to be some fairy tale."

He smiled slowly, his green eyes lighting with a promise as his hand slid away. "It can be."

Without another word, he leaned back and closed his eyes. Going to sleep? Her whole body was on fire from his touch, his words—his seduction. And he'd simply gone to sleep. She wanted to shout in frustration.

Worse yet, she wanted him to recline her back on the sofa and make love to her as thoroughly as he'd done eleven months ago.

Six

By nightfall in Spain, Elliot wondered how Lucy Ann would react to their lodgings for the night. The limousine wound deeper into the historic district, farther from the racetrack than they normally stayed. But he had new ideas for these next few weeks, based on what Lucy Ann had said on the plane.

After the fairy-tale discussion, inspiration had struck. He'd forced himself to make a tactical retreat so he could regroup. Best not to risk pushing her further and having her shut him down altogether before he could put his plan into action to persuade her to stay longer than the month.

Once she was tucked into the back room on the airplane to nurse Eli, Elliot had made a few calls and set the wheels in motion to change their accommodations along the way. A large bank account and a hefty dose of fame worked wonders for making things happen fast. He just hoped his new agenda would impress Lucy Ann. Winning her over was becoming more pressing by the second. Not just for Eli but because Elliot's life had been damn empty without her. He hadn't realized just how much until he had her back. The way her presence made everything around him more vibrant. Hell, even her organized nature, which he used to tease her about. She brought a focus, a grounding and a beauty to his world that he didn't want to lose again.

Failure was not an option.

He'd made himself a checklist, just like he kept for his work. People thought he was impulsive, reckless even, but there was a science to his job. Mathematics. Calculations. He studied all the details and contingencies until they became so deeply ingrained they were instinct.

Still, he refused to become complacent. He reviewed that checklist before every race as if he were a rookie driver. Now he needed to apply the same principles to winning back Lucy Ann's friendship...and more.

Their new "hotel" took shape on the top of the hill, the Spanish sunset adding the perfect dusky aura to their new accommodations.

In the seat across from him, Lucy Ann sat up straighter, looking from the window to him with confusion stamped on her lovely face.

"This isn't where you usually stay. This is...a castle."

"Exactly."

The restored medieval castle provided safety and space, privacy and romance. He could give her the fairy tale while making sure Lucy Ann and their son were protected. He could—and would—provide all the things a real partner and father provided. He would be everything his father wasn't.

"Change of plans for our stay."

"Because...?"

"We need more space and less chance of interruptions." He couldn't wait to have her all to himself. Damn, he'd missed her.

"But pandering to the paparazzi plays an important role in your PR." She hugged the diaper bag closer to her chest; the baby's bag, her camera and her computer had been the only things she'd insisted on bringing with her from home.

"Pandering?" He forced himself to focus on her words rather than the sound of her voice. Her lyrical Southern drawl was like honey along his starved senses. "That's not a word I'm particularly comfortable with. Playing along with them, perhaps. Regardless, they don't own me, and I absolutely will not allow them to have access to you and our son on anything other than our own terms."

"Wow, okay." Her eyes went wide before she grinned wryly. "But did you have to rent a castle?"

He wondered if he'd screwed up by going overboard, but her smile reassured him he'd struck gold by surprising her.

"It's a castle converted to a hotel, although yes, it's more secure and roomier." Safer, but also with romantic overtones he hoped would score points. "I thought in each place we stay, we could explore a different option for traveling with a child."

"This is…an interesting option," she conceded as the limousine cruised along the sweeping driveway leading up to the towering stone castle. Ivy scrolled up toward the turrets, the walls beneath baked brown with time. Only a few more minutes and the chauffeur would open the door.

Elliot chose his words wisely to set the stage before they went inside. "Remember how when we were kids, we hid in the woods and tossed blankets over branches? I called them forts, but you called them castles. I was cool with that as long as I got to be a knight rather than some pansy prince."

They'd climbed into those castle forts where he'd read for hours while she colored or drew pictures.

"Pansy prince?" She chuckled, tapping his chest. "You *are* anti-fairy-tale. What happened to the kid who used to lose himself in storybooks?"

He captured her finger and held on for a second before linking hands. "There are knights in fairy tales. And there are definitely castles."

"Is that what this is about?" She left her hand in his. "Showing me a fairy tale?"

"Think about coming here in the future with Eli." He stared at his son's sleeping face and images filled his head of their child walking, playing, a toddler with his hair and Lucy Ann's freckles. "Our son can pretend to be a knight or a prince, whatever he chooses, in a real castle. How freaking cool is that?"

"Very cool." A smile teased her kissable pink lips. "But this place is a long way from our tattered quilt forts in the woods."

His own smile faded. "Different from our childhood is a very good thing."

Her whole body swayed toward him, and she cupped his face. "Elliot, it's good that our child won't suffer the way we did, but what your father did to you...that had nothing to do with money."

Lucy Ann's sympathy, the pain for him that shone in her eyes, rocked the ground under him. He needed to regain control. He'd left that part of his life behind and he had no desire to revisit it even in his thoughts. So he deflected as he always did, keeping things light.

"I like it when you get prissy." He winked. "That's really sexy."

"Elliot, this isn't the time to joke around. We have some very serious decisions to make this month."

"I'm completely serious. Cross my heart." He pressed their clasped hands against his chest. "It makes me want to ruffle your feathers."

"Stop. It." She tugged free. "We're talking about Eli. Not us."

"That's why we're at a castle, for Eli," he insisted as the limousine stopped in front of the sprawling fortress. "Einstein said, 'The true sign of intelligence is not knowledge but imagination.' That's what we can offer our son with this unique lifestyle. The opportunity to explore his imagination around the world, to see those things that we only read about. You don't have to answer. Just think on it while we're here."

With the baby nursing, Lucy Ann curled up in her massive bed. She took comfort in the routine of feeding her child, the sweet softness of his precious cheek against her breast. With her life turning upside down so fast, she needed something familiar to hold on to.

The medieval decor wrapped her in a timeless fantasy she wasn't quite sure how to deal with. The castle had tapestries on the wall and sconces with bulbs that flickered like flames. Her four-poster bed had heavy drapes around it, the wooden pillars as thick as any warrior's chest. An arm's reach away waited a bassinet, a shiny reproduction of an antique wooden cradle for Eli.

Her eyes gravitated toward the tapestry across the room telling a love story about a knight romancing a maiden by a river. Elliot had chosen well. She couldn't help but be charmed by this place. Even her supper was served authentically in a trencher, with water in a goblet.

A plush, woven rug on the stone floor, along with

the low snap of the fire in the hearth, kept out the chilly spring night. The sound system piped madrigal music as if the group played in a courtyard below.

Through the slightly opened door, she saw the sitting room where Elliot was parked at a desk, his computer in front of him. Reviewing stats on his competitors? Or a million other details related to the racing season? She missed being a part of all that, but he had a new assistant, a guy who did his job so seamlessly he blended into the background.

And speaking of work, she had some of her own to complete. Once Eli finished nursing and went to bed there would be nothing for her to do but complete the two projects she hadn't been able to put on hold.

She'd expected Elliot to try to make a move on her once they got inside, but the suite had three bedrooms off the living area. One for her and one for him. The British nanny he'd hired had settled into the third, turning in after Lucy Ann made it clear Eli would stay with his mother tonight. While Mrs. Clayworth kept a professional face in place, the furrows along her forehead made it clear that she wondered at the lack of work on this job.

This whole setup delivered everything Elliot had promised, a unique luxury she could see her son enjoying someday. Any family would relish these fairy-tale accommodations. It was beyond tempting.

Elliot was beyond tempting.

Lucy Ann tore her eyes from her lifetime friend and onetime lover. This month was going to be a lot more difficult than she'd anticipated.

Desperate for some grounding in reality before she weakened, she reached for her phone, for the present, and called her aunt Carla.

* * *

She'd made it through the night, even if the covers on the bed behind her were a rumpled mess from her restless tossing and turning.

Lucy Ann sat at the desk at the tower window with her laptop, grateful to Carla for the bolstering. Too bad she couldn't come join them on this trip, but Carla was emphatic. She loved her home and her life. She was staying where she belonged.

Who could blame her? A sense of belonging was a rare gift Lucy Ann hadn't quite figured out how to capture yet. In South Carolina, she'd dreamed of getting out, and here she craved the familiarity of home.

Which made her feel like a total ingrate.

She was living the easy life, one any new mother would embrace. How ironic that at home she'd spent every day exhausted, feeling like Eli's naps were always a few minutes too short to accomplish what she needed to do. And now, she spent most of her time waiting for him to wake up.

She closed her laptop, caught up on work, dressed for the day, waiting to leave for Elliot's race. She still couldn't wrap her brain around how different this trip was from ones she'd shared with Elliot in the past. Staring out the window in their tower suite, she watched the sun cresting higher over the manicured grounds.

Last night, she'd actually slept in a castle. The restored structure was the epitome of luxury and history all rolled into one. She'd even pulled out her camera and snapped some photos to use for a client's web design. Her fingers already itched to get to the computer and play with the images, but Elliot was due back soon.

He'd gone to the track for prelim work, his race scheduled for tomorrow. Normally he arrived even earlier before an event, but the wedding had muddled his schedule. God, she hoped his concentration was rock solid. The thought of him in a wreck because she'd damaged his focus sent her stomach roiling. Why hadn't she considered this before? She should have told him about Eli earlier for so many reasons.

She was familiar with everything about his work world. She'd been his personal assistant for over a decade, in charge of every detail of his career, his life. And even in their time apart she'd kept up with him and the racing world online. Formula One racing in Spain alternated locations every year, Barcelona to Valencia and back again. She knew his preferences for routes like Valencia, with the street track bordering the harbor. She was used to being busy, in charge—not sitting around a castle twiddling her thumbs, eating fruit and cheese from medieval pottery.

Being waited on by staff, nannies and chauffeurs, being at loose ends, felt alien, to say the least. But she'd agreed to give him a chance this month. She would stick to her word.

As if conjured from her thoughts, Elliot appeared in the arched doorway between the living area and her bedroom. Jeans hugged his lean hips, his turtleneck shirt hugging a well-defined chest. Her mouth watered as she considered what he would do if she walked across the room, leaned against his chest to kiss him, tucked her hands in his back pockets and savored the chemistry simmering between them.

She swallowed hard. "Are you here for lunch?"

"I'm here for you and Eli." He held out a cashmere sweater of his. "In case you get chilly on our outing."

"Outing?" she asked to avoid taking the sweater until she could figure out what to do next.

She'd worn pieces of Elliot's clothes countless times over the years without a second thought, but the notion of wrapping his sweater around her now felt so intimate that desire pooled between her legs. However, to reject the sweater would make an issue of it, revealing feelings that made her too vulnerable, a passion she still didn't know how to control yet.

Gingerly, she took the sweater from him, the cashmere still warm from his touch. "Where are we going?"

He smiled mysteriously. "It's another surprise for you and Eli."

"Can't I even have a hint?" She hugged the sweater close, finding she was enjoying his game more than she should.

"We're going to play." He scooped his son up from the cradle in sure hands. "Right, Eli, buddy? We're going to take good care of your mama today. If she agrees to come with me, of course."

The sight of their son cradled in Elliot's broad hands brought her heart into her throat. She'd imagined moments like this, dreamed of how she would introduce him to their child. Day after day, her plan had altered as she delayed yet again.

And why? Truly, why? She still wasn't sure she understood why she'd made all the decisions she'd made these past months. She needed to use her time wisely to figure out the best way to navigate their future.

She tugged on the sweater. "Who am I to argue with such a tempting offer? Let's go play."

They left the suite and traveled down the sweeping stone stairway without a word, passing other guests as well as the staff dressed in period garb. The massive front doors even creaked as they swept open to reveal the waiting limousine.

Stepping out into the sunshine, she took in the incredible lawns. The modern-day buzz of cars and airplanes mixed with the historical landscaping that followed details down to the drawbridge over a moat.

The chauffeur opened the limo door for her. Lucy Ann slid inside, then extended her arms for her child. Elliot passed over Eli as easily as if they were a regular family.

Lucy Ann hugged her son close for a second, breathing in the baby-powder-fresh scent of him before securing Eli into his car seat. "Shouldn't you be preparing for race day?"

Getting his head together. Resting. Focusing.

"I know what I need to do," he answered as if reading her mind. He sat across from her, his long legs extended, his eyes holding hers. "That doesn't mean we can't have time together today."

"I don't want to be the cause of your exhaustion or lack of focus because you felt the need to entertain me." She'd been so hurt and angry for a year, she'd lost sight of other feelings. Race day was exciting and terrifying at the same time. "I've been a part of your world for too long to let you be reckless."

"Trust me. I have more reason than ever to be careful. You and Eli are my complete and total focus now."

There was no mistaking the certainty and resolve in his voice. Her fears eased somewhat, which made room for her questions about the day to come back to the fore. "At least tell me something about your plans for today. Starting with, where are we going?"

He leaned to open the minifridge and pulled out two water bottles. "Unless you object, we are going to the San Miguel de los Reyes Monastery."

She sat up straighter, surprised, intrigued. She took

the water bottle from him. "I'm not sure I understand your plan…."

"The monastery has been converted into a library. We've never had a chance to visit before on other trips." He twisted open his spring water. "In fact, as I look back, we both worked nonstop, all the time. As I reevaluate, I'm realizing now a little sightseeing won't set us behind."

"That's certainly a one-eighty from the past. You've always been a very driven man—no pun intended." She smiled at her halfhearted joke, feeling more than a little off balance by this change in Elliot. "I'll just say thank-you. This is a very thoughtful idea. Although I'm curious. What made you decide on this particular outing when there are so many more obvious tourist sites we haven't visited?"

"You sparked the idea when we were on the airplane, actually." He rolled the bottle between his palms. "You mentioned not believing in fairy tales anymore. That is why I chose the castle. Fairy tales are important for any kid…and I think we've both lost sight of that."

"We're adults." With adult wants and needs. Like the need to peel off his forest-green turtleneck and faded jeans.

"Even as kids, we were winging it with those fairy tales. Then we both grew jaded so young." He shrugged muscular shoulders. "So it's time for us to learn more about fairy tales so we can be good parents. Speaking of which, is Eli buckled in?"

"Of course."

"Good." He tapped on the window for the chauffeur to go. "Just in case you were wondering, I'm calling this the *Beauty and the Beast* plan."

They were honest-to-goodness going to a library. She sagged back, stunned and charmed all at once.

God, she thought she'd seen all his moves over the years—moves he'd used on other women. He'd always been more…boisterous. More obvious.

This was different. Subtle. Damn good.

"So I'm to be Belle to your beast."

"A Southern belle, yes, and you've called me a beast in the past. Besides, you know how much I enjoy books and history. I thought you might find some interesting photo opportunities along the way."

"You really are okay with a pedestrian stroll through a library." The Elliot she'd known all her life had always been on the go, scaling the tallest tree, racing down the steepest hill, looking for the edgiest challenge. But he did enjoy unwinding with a good book, too. She forgot about that side of him sometimes.

"I'm not a Cro-Magnon…even though I'm playing the beast. I do read. I even use a napkin at dinnertime." He waggled his eyebrows at her, his old playful nature more evident.

She wished she could have just slugged him on the shoulder as if they were thirteen again. Things had been simpler then on some levels—and yet not easy at all on others.

"You're right. I shouldn't have been surprised."

"Let's stop making assumptions about each other from now on about a lot of things. We've been friends for years, but even friends change, grow, even a man like me can mature when he's ready. Thanks to you and Eli, I'm ready now."

She wanted to believe him, to believe in him. She wanted to shake off a past where the people she cared about always let her down. Hundreds of times over the past eleven months she'd guessed at what his reaction would be if she told him about the baby.

She'd known he would come through for her. The part that kept haunting her, that kept her from trying... She could never figure out how she would know if he'd come through out of duty or something more.

The thought that she could yearn for more between the two of them scared her even now. She was much better off taking this one day at a time.

"Okay, Elliot—" she spread her arms wide "—I'm all-in...for our day at the monastery."

As she settled in for her date, she couldn't help wondering which was tougher: resisting the fairy-tale man who seemed content to ignore the past year or facing the reality of her lifelong friend who had every reason to be truly angry with her.

Regardless, at some point the past would catch up with both of them. They could only play games for so long before they had to deal with their shared parenthood.

Wearing a baseball cap with the brim tugged low, Elliot soaked in the sight of Lucy Ann's appreciation of the frescoes and ancient tomes as she filled a memory card with photos of the monastery turned library. He should have thought to do this for her sooner. The place was relatively deserted, a large facility with plenty of places for tourists to spread out. A school tour had passed earlier, but the echoes of giggles had faded thirty minutes ago. No one recognized him, and the bodyguards hung back unobtrusively. For all intents and purposes, he and Lucy Ann were just a regular family on vacation.

Why had he never thought to bring her to places like this before? He'd convinced himself he was taking care of her by offering her a job and a life following him around the world. But somehow he'd missed out on giving her so much more. He'd let her down when they were teenagers and he'd gotten arrested, leaving her alone to deal with her family. Now to find out he'd been selfish as an adult too. That didn't sit well with him.

So he had more to fix. He and Lucy Ann were bound by their child for life, but he didn't intend to take that part for granted. He would work his tail off to be more for her this time.

He set the brake on the stroller by a looming marble angel. "You're quiet. Anything I can get for you?"

She glanced away from her camera, looking back over her shoulder at him. "Everything's perfect. Thank you. I'm enjoying the peace. And the frescoes as well as the ornately bound books. This was a wonderful idea for how to spend the afternoon."

Yet all day long she'd kept that camera between them, snapping photos. For work? For pleasure?

Or to keep from looking at him?

Tired of the awkward silence, he pushed on, "If you're having fun, then why aren't you smiling?"

She lowered the camera slowly, pivoting to face him. Her eyes were wary. "I'm not sure what you mean."

"Lucy Ann, it's me here. Elliot. Can we pretend it's fifteen years ago and just be honest with each other?"

She nibbled her bottom lip for a moment before blurting out, "I appreciate what you're doing, that you're trying, but I keep waiting for the explosion."

He scratched over his closely shorn hair, which brought memories of sprinting away from a burning car. "I thought we cleared that up in the limo. I'm not going to wreck tomorrow."

"And I'm not talking about that now." She tucked the camera away slowly, pausing as an older couple meandered past looking at a brochure map of the museum. Once they cleared the small chapel area, she turned back to him and said softly, "I'm talking about an explosion of anger. You have to be mad at me for not telling you about Eli sooner. I accept that it was wrong of me not to try harder. I just keep wondering when the argument will happen."

God, was she really expecting him to go ballistic on her? He would never, never be like his father. He used his racing as an outlet for those aggressive feelings. He did what he needed to do to stay in control. Always.

Maybe he wasn't as focused as he claimed to be, because if he'd been thinking straight he would have realized that Lucy Ann would misunderstand. She'd spent her life on shaky ground growing up, her mother hooking up with a different boyfriend or husband every week. Beyond that, she'd always stepped in for others, a quiet warrior in her own right.

"You always did take the blame for things."

"What does that have to do with today?"

He gestured for her to sit on a pew, then joined her. "When we were kids, you took the blame for things I did—like breaking the aquarium and letting the snake loose in the school."

She smiled nostalgically. "And cutting off Sharilynn's braid. Not a nice thing to do at all, by the way."

"She was mean to you. She deserved it." He and Lucy Ann had been each other's champions in those days. "But you shouldn't have told the teacher you did it. You ended up cleaning the erasers for a week."

"I enjoyed staying after school. And my mom didn't do anything except laugh, then make me write an apology and do some extra chores." She looked down at her hands twisted in her lap. "Your father wouldn't have laughed if the school called him."

"You're right there." He scooped up her hand and held

on. It was getting easier and easier for them to be together again. As much as he hated revisiting the past, if it worked to bring her back into his life, he would walk over hot coals in hell for her. "You protected me every bit as much as I tried to protect you."

"But your risk was so much higher...with your dad." She squeezed his hand. "You did the knightly thing. That meant a lot to a scrawny girl no one noticed except to make fun of her clothes or her mom."

He looked up at Lucy Ann quickly. Somehow he'd forgotten that part of her past. He always saw her as quietly feisty. "What elementary school boy cares about someone's clothes?"

"True enough, I guess." She studied him through the sweep of long eyelashes. "I never quite understood why you decided we would be friends—before we started taking the blame for each other's transgressions."

Why? He thought back to that time, to the day he saw her sitting at the computer station, her legs swinging, too short to reach the ground. The rest of the class was running around their desks while the teacher stepped out to speak with a parent. "You were peaceful. I wasn't. We balanced each other out. We can have that again."

"You're pushing." She tugged her hand.

He held firm. "Less than a minute ago, you told me I have the right to be mad at you."

"And I have the right to apologize and walk away."

Her quick retort surprised him. The Lucy Ann of the past would have been passive rather than confrontational. Like leaving for a year and having his baby. "Yeah, you're good at that, avoiding."

"There." She looked up quickly. "Tell me off. Be angry. Do anything other than smile and pretend everything's okay between us while we tour around the world like some dream couple."

Her fire bemused him and mesmerized him. "You are the most confusing woman I have ever met."

"Good." She stood up quickly, tugging her camera bag back onto her shoulder. "Women have always fallen into your arms far too easily. Time to finish the tour."

Seven

Lucy Ann swaddled her son in a fluffy towel after his bath while the nanny, Mrs. Clayworth, placed a fresh diaper and sleeper on the changing table. After the full day touring, then dinner with the nanny so Lucy Ann could get to know her better, she felt more comfortable with the woman.

Elliot's thoughtfulness and care for their son's future touched her. He'd charmed Mrs. Clayworth, yet asked perceptive questions. The woman appeared soft and like someone out of a Disney movie, but over the hours it became clear she was more than a stereotype. More than a résumé as a pediatric nurse. She was an avid musician and a hiker who enjoyed the world travel that came with her job. She spent her days off trekking through different local sites or attending concerts.

Lucy Ann liked the woman more and more with every

minute that passed. "Mrs. Clayworth, so you really were a nanny for royalty? That had to have been exciting."

Her eyes twinkled as she held out her arms for Eli. "You have seen my list of references. But that's just about the parents." She tucked Eli against her shoulder with expert hands, patting his back. "A baby doesn't care anything about lineage or credentials. Only that he or she is dry, fed, cuddled and loved."

"I can see clearly enough that you have a gift with babies."

The nanny's patience had been admirable when, just after supper, Eli cried himself purple over a bout of gas.

"I had two of my own. The child care career started once they left for the university. I used to be a pediatric nurse and while the money was good, it wasn't enough. I had bills to pay because of my loser ex-husband, and thanks to my daughter's connections with a blue-blooded roommate, I lucked into a career I thoroughly enjoy."

Having lived the past months as a single mom, Lucy Ann sympathized. Except she had always had the safety net of calling Elliot. She'd had her aunt's help, as well. What if she'd had nowhere to go and no one's help? The thought made her stomach knot with apprehension. That didn't mean she would stay with Elliot just because of her bills—but she certainly needed to make more concrete plans.

"I want the best for my son, too."

"Well, as much as I like my job, you have to know the best can't always be bought with money."

So very true. Lucy Ann took Eli back to dress him in his teddy bear sleeper. "You remind me of my aunt."

"I hope that's a compliment." She tucked the towel into the laundry chute.

"It is. Aunt Carla is my favorite relative." Not that

there was a lot of stiff competition. She traced the appliquéd teddy bear on the pj's and thought of her aunt's closet full of themed clothes. "She always wears these chipper seasonal T-shirts and sweatshirts. She has a thick Southern accent and deep-fries everything, including pickles. I know on the outside it sounds like the two of you are nothing alike, but on the inside, there's a calming spirit about you both."

"Then I will most certainly take that as a compliment, love." She walked to the pitcher on the desk by the window and poured a glass of water. "I respect that you're taking your time to get to know me and to see how I handle your son. Not all parents are as careful with their wee ones."

Mrs. Clayworth placed the glass beside the ornately carved rocker thoughtfully, even though Lucy Ann hadn't mentioned how thirsty she got when she nursed Eli. Money couldn't buy happiness, but having extra hands sure made life easier. She snapped Eli's sleeper up to his neck.

"I do trust Elliot's judgment. I've known him all my life. We've relied on each other for so much." There had been a time when she thought there was nothing he could do that would drive a wedge between them. "Except now there's this new dynamic to adjust to with Eli. But then you probably see that all the time."

Lucy Ann scooped up her son and settled into the wooden rocker, hoping she wasn't the only new mother to have conflicted feelings about her role. As much as she loved nursing her baby, she couldn't deny the occasional twinge of sadness that the same body Elliot once touched with passion had been relegated to a far more utilitarian purpose.

"You're a new mum." Mrs. Clayworth passed a burp cloth. "That's a huge and blessed change."

"My own mother wasn't much of a role model." She adjusted her shirt, and Eli hungrily latched on.

"And this favorite aunt of yours?" The nanny adjusted the bedding in the cradle, draping a fresh blanket over the end, before taking on the many other countless details in wrapping up the day.

"She helped as much as she could, but my mother resented the connection sometimes." Especially when her mom was between boyfriends and lonely. Then suddenly it wasn't so convenient to have Lucy Ann hang out with Aunt Carla. "I've been reading everything I can find on parenting. I even took some classes at the hospital, but there are too many things to cover in books or courses."

"Amen, dear."

Having this woman to lean on was…incredible, to say the least. Elliot was clearly working the fairy tale–like life from all angles.

She would be pridefully foolish to ignore the resources this woman brought to the table. Isolating herself for the past eleven months had been a mistake. Lucy Ann needed to correct that tendency and find balance. She needed to learn to accept help and let others into her life. Starting now seemed like a good idea.

She couldn't deny that all this "playing house" with Elliot was beginning to chip away at her reservations and her resolve to keep her distance. Elliot had said they needed to use this time to figure out how to parent Eli. She knew now they also needed to use this time to learn how to be in the same room with each other without melting into a pool of hormones. Time to quit running from the attraction and face it. Deal with it.

"And that's where your experience comes in. I would

be foolish not to learn from you." Lucy Ann paused, patting Eli's pedaling feet. "Why do you look so surprised?"

"Mothers seek help from me, not advice. You are a unique one."

"Would you mind staying for a while so we can talk?"

"Of course. I don't mind at all."

Lucy Ann gestured to the wingback chair on the other side of the fireplace. "I'd like to ask you a few questions."

"About babies?" she asked, sitting.

"Nope, I'd like to ask your advice on men."

The winner's trophy always felt so good in his hands, but today…the victory felt hollow in comparison with what he really wanted. More time with Lucy Ann.

Elliot held the trophy high with one hand, his helmet tucked under his other arm.

His *Beauty and the Beast* plan had gone well. They'd spent a low-key day together. Her pensive expression gave him hope he was on the right path. If she was ready to check out and return to Columbia, there would have been decisiveness on her face. But he was making headway with her. He could see that. He just needed to keep pushing forward with his plans, steady on. And try like hell to ignore the urge to kiss her every second they were together.

A wiry reporter pushed a microphone forward through the throng of fans and press all shouting congratulations. "Mr. Starc, tell us about the new lady in your life."

"Is it true she was your former assistant?"

"Where has she been this year?"

"Did she quit or was she fired?"

"Lovers' spat?"

"Which designer deserves credit for her makeover?"

Makeover? What the hell were they talking about?

To him, she was Lucy Ann—always pretty and special. And even though she had come out of her shell some in the past year, that didn't change the core essence of her, the woman he'd always known and admired.

Sure, her new curves added a bombshell quality. And the clothes his new assistant had ordered were flashier. None of that mattered to him. He'd wanted her before. He wanted her still.

The wiry reporter shoved the mic closer. "Are you sure the baby is yours?"

That question pulled him up short in anger. "I understand that the press thinks the personal life of anyone with a little fame is fair game. But when it comes to my family, I will not tolerate slanderous statements. If you want access to me, you will respect my son and his mother. And now it's time for me to celebrate with my family. Interviews are over."

He heard his assistant hiss in protest over the way he'd handled the question. The paparazzi expected to be fed, not spanked.

Shouldering through the crowd, Elliot kept his eyes locked on Lucy Ann in his private box, watching. Had she heard the questions through the speaker box? He hoped not. He didn't want anything to mar the evening he had planned. She'd actually consented to let the nanny watch Eli. Elliot would have her all to himself.

He kept walking, pushing through the throng.

"Congratulations, Starc," another reporter persisted. "How are you planning to celebrate?"

"How long do you expect your winning streak to run?"

"Is the woman and your kid the reason your engagement broke off?"

He continued to "no comment" his way all the way up the steps, into a secure hallway and to the private viewing box in the grandstand where Lucy Ann waited with a couple of honored guests, local royalty and politicians he only just managed to acknowledge with a quick greeting and thanks for attending. His entire focus locked on Lucy Ann.

"You won," she squealed, her smile enveloping him every bit as much as if she'd hugged him. Her red wraparound dress clung to her body, outlining every curve.

He would give up his trophy in a heartbeat to tug that tie with his teeth until her dress fell open.

"I think we should go." Before he embarrassed them both in front of reporters and esteemed guests.

He couldn't wait to get her alone. All he'd been able to think about during the race was getting back to Lucy Ann so he could continue his campaign. Move things closer to the point where he could kiss her as he wanted.

"Right." She leaned to pluck her purse from her seat. "The after-parties."

"Not tonight," he said softly for her ears only. "I have other plans."

"You have responsibilities to your career. I understand that."

He pulled her closer, whispering, "The press is particularly ravenous today. We need to go through the private elevator."

Her eyebrows pinched together. "I'm not so sure that's the best idea."

Damn it, was she going to bail on him before he even had a chance to get started? He would just have to figure out a way around it. "What do you propose we do instead?"

She tugged his arm, the warmth of her touch reaching through his race jacket as she pulled him closer to the observation window. "You taught me long ago that the best way to get rid of the hungry press is to feed them tidbits."

The tip of her tongue touched her top lip briefly before she arched up on her toes to kiss him. He stood stock-still in shock for a second before—hell, yeah—he was all-in. His arms banded around her waist. She leaned into him, looping her arms his neck. He could almost imagine the cameras clicking as fast as his heartbeat, picking up speed with every moment he had Lucy Ann in his arms.

He didn't know what had changed her mind, but he was damn glad.

Her fingers played along his hair and he remembered the feel of her combing her hands through it the night they'd made love. He'd kept his hair longer then, before the accident.

Lucy Ann sighed into his mouth as she began to pull back with a smile. "That should keep the media vultures happy for a good long while." She nipped his bottom lip playfully before asking, "Are you ready to celebrate your win?"

Lucy Ann stepped out onto the castle balcony, the night air cool, the stone flooring under her feet even cooler but not cold enough to send her back inside. She walked to the half wall along the balcony and let the breeze lift her hair and ruffle through her dress before turning back to the table.

Elliot was showering off the scent of gasoline. He'd already ordered supper. The meal waited for them, savory Spanish spices drifting along the air.

There was no question that Elliot had ordered the dinner spread personally. The table was laden with her favorites, right down to a flan for dessert. Elliot remembered. She'd spent so much time as his assistant making sure to remember every detail of his life, she hadn't considered he'd been paying just as close attention to her.

She trailed her fingers along the edge of her water goblet. The sounds below—other guests coming and going, laughing and talking—mingled with the sound system wafting more madrigal tunes into the night. She didn't even have the nursery monitor with her for the first time since... She couldn't remember when. Mrs. Clayworth had already planned to watch Eli tonight since Lucy Ann had expected to go to an after-race party with Elliot.

Then she'd kissed him.

Halfway through that impulsive gesture, Lucy Ann realized that holding back was no longer an option. Sleeping with Elliot again was all but inevitable. The longer she waited, the more intense the fallout would be. They needed to figure out this crazy attraction now, while their son was still young enough not to know if things didn't work out.

Her stomach knotted with nerves. But the attraction was only getting stronger the longer she denied herself. It was only a matter of time—

As if conjured from that wish, Elliot stood in the balcony doorway, so fresh from the shower his short hair still held a hint of water. He'd changed into simple black pants and a white shirt with the sleeves rolled up. With the night shadows and flickering sconce lights he had a timeless air—the Elliot from the past mixing with the man he'd become.

She wanted them both.

Lucy Ann swallowed nervously and searched for something to say to break the crackling silence between them. "I can't believe the press actually left us alone after the race."

"We did slip away out a back entrance."

"That never stopped them before."

"I ordered extra security." He stalked toward her slowly. "I don't want anyone hassling you or Eli. Our lives are private now. I'm done playing the paparazzi game. At least we know this place is secure."

"As private as the woods we hid in as kids."

How many times had he made her feel safe? As if those quilted walls could hold out the world while they huddled inside reading books and coloring pictures like regular kids.

He stopped in front of her, his hand brushing back a stray lock of her hair. "Why did you kiss me after the race?"

"To keep the press content." To let other women know he was taken? "Because I wanted to."

He tugged the lock of hair lightly. "I meant why did you bite me?"

A laugh rolled free and rode the breeze. "Oh, that. Can't have everything going your way."

"You're more confident these days." His emerald eyes glinted with curiosity—and promise.

"Motherhood has given me purpose." Even now, the need to settle her life for her child pushed her to move faster with Elliot, to figure out one way or another.

To take what she could from this time together in case everything imploded later.

"I like seeing you more comfortable in your skin." He sat on the balcony half wall with unerring balance and confidence. "Letting the rest of the world see the woman you are."

As much as she feared trusting a man—trusting Elliot—she couldn't help but wonder if he would continue trying to spin a fairy-tale future for them long beyond tonight and ignore the fact that she had been the unnoticed Cinderella all her life. She wanted a man who noticed the real her—not the fairy tale. Not the fantasy. If she was honest, she was still afraid his sexual interest had come too late to feel authentic.

"You make me sound like I was a mouse before—someone in need of a makeover, like that reporter said."

He cursed softly. "You heard their questions?"

"The TV system in the private box was piping in feed from the winner's circle." She rolled her eyes. "It was a backhanded compliment of sorts."

"Don't ever forget I saw the glow long before."

She couldn't help but ask, "If you saw my glow, then why did it take you all those years to make a move on me?"

"If I remember correctly, you made the first move."

She winced, some of her confidence fading at the thought that they could have still been just friends if she hadn't impulsively kissed him that night they'd been drunk, celebrating and nostalgic. "Thanks for reminding me how I made a fool of myself."

"You're misunderstanding." He linked fingers with her, tugging her closer. "I've always found you attractive, but you were off-limits. Something much more valuable than a lover—those are a dime a dozen. You were, you are, my friend."

She wanted to believe him. "A dime a dozen. Nice."

"Lucy Ann, stop." He squeezed her hand. "I don't want to fight with you. It doesn't have to be that way for us this time. Trust me. I have a plan."

She'd planned to seduce him, keep things light, and he was going serious on her. She tried to lighten the mood again. "What fairy tale does this night come from?"

"It could be reality."

"You disappoint me." She leaned closer until their

chests just brushed. Her breasts beaded in response. "Tonight, I want the fairy tale."

He blinked in surprise. "Okay, fair enough." He stood, tugging her to the middle of the balcony. "We're in the middle of Cinderella's ball."

Appropriate, given her thoughts earlier. "Well, the clock is definitely ticking since Eli still wakes up in the middle of the night."

"Then we should make the most of this evening." The moonlight cast a glow around them, adding to the magical air of the night. "Are you ready for supper?"

"Honestly?" She swayed in time with the classical music.

"I wouldn't have asked if I hadn't wanted to know. I don't think you know how much I want to make you happy."

She stepped closer, lifting their hands. "Then let's dance."

"I can accommodate." He brought her hand to rest on his shoulder, his palm sliding warmly along her waist. "I owe you for homecoming our sophomore year in high school. You had that pretty dress your aunt made. She showed me so I could make sure the flowers on your wrist corsage matched just the right shade of blue."

"I can't believe you still remember about a high school dance." Or that he remembered the color of her dress.

"I got arrested for car theft and stood you up." He rested his chin on top of her head. "That tends to make a night particularly memorable."

"I knew it was really your friends that night, not you."

He angled back to look in her warm chocolate-brown eyes. "Why didn't you tell me you thought that?"

"You would have argued with me about some technical detail." She teased, all the while too aware of the freshly showered scent of him. "You were even more stubborn in those days."

"I *did* steal that car." He tugged her closer and stole her breath so she couldn't speak. "And it wasn't a technicality. I wanted to take you to the dance in decent wheels. I figured the used car dealership would never know as long as I returned it in the morning."

"I wouldn't have cared what kind of car we had that night."

"I know. But I cared. And ended up spending the night in jail before the car dealer dismissed the charges—God only knows why." He laughed darkly. "That night in jail was the best night's sleep I'd gotten in a long time, being out of my father's house."

God, he was breaking her heart. Their childhoods were so damaged, had they even stood a chance at a healthy adult relationship with each other? She rested her head on his shoulder and let him talk, taking in the steady beat of his pulse to help steady her own.

"I felt like such a bastard for sleeping, for being grateful for a night's break from my dad when I'd let you down."

Let her down? He'd been her port in the storm, her safe harbor. "Elliot," she said softly, "it was a silly dance. I was more worried about how your father would react to your arrest."

"I wanted to give you everything," he said, ignoring her comment about his dad. "But I let you down time after time."

This conversation was straying so far from her plans for seduction, her plans to work out the sensual ache inside her. "This isn't the sort of thing Prince Charming says to Cinderella at the ball."

"My point is that I'm trying to give you everything

now, if you'll just let me." He nuzzled her hair. "Just tell me what you want."

Every cell in her body shouted for her to say she wanted him to peel off her dress and make love to her against the castle wall. Instead, she found herself whispering, "All I want is for Eli to be happy and to lead a normal life."

"You think this isn't normal." His feet matched steps with hers as the music flowed into their every move.

A castle? A monastery library? "Well, this isn't your average trip to a bookstore or corner library, that's for sure."

"There are playgrounds here as well as libraries. We just have to find them for Eli."

Lucy Ann felt a stab of guilt. Elliot was thinking of their son and she'd been thinking about sex. "You make it sound so simple."

"It can be."

If only she could buy into his notion of keeping things simple long-term. "Except I never contacted you about being pregnant."

"And I didn't come after you like I should have. I let my pride get stung, and hurt another woman in the process."

She hadn't considered the fact that Gianna had been wronged in this situation. "What happens in the future if you find someone else…or if I do?"

"You want monogamy?" he asked. "I can do that."

"You say that so quickly, but you're also the one spinning fairy tales and games." She looked up at him. "I'm asking honest questions now."

She wondered why she was pushing so hard for answers to questions that could send him running. Was she on a self-destructive path in spite of her plans to be with him? Then again, this level of honesty between them had been a long time coming.

His feet stopped. He cupped her face until their eyes met. "Believe this. You're the only woman I want. You're sure as hell more woman than I can handle, so if you will stay with me, then monogamy is a piece of cake."

"Are you proposing?"

"I'm proposing we stay together, sleep together, be friends, lovers, parents."

He wasn't proposing. This wasn't Cinderella's ball after all. They were making an arrangement of convenience—to enjoy sex and friendship.

She didn't believe in fairy tales, damn it. So she should take exactly what he offered. But she intended to make sure he understood that convenience did not mean she would simply follow his lead.

Eight

Lucy Ann stepped out of his arms, and a protest roared inside Elliot. Damn it, was she leaving? Rejecting him in spite of everything they'd just said to each other? He set his jaw and stuffed his hands into his pockets to keep from turning into an idiot, a fool begging her to stay.

Except she didn't move any farther away. She locked eyes with him, her pupils wide—from the dark or from desire? He sure as hell hoped for the latter. Her hand went to the tie of her silky wraparound dress and she tugged.

His jaw dropped. "Um, Lucy Ann? Are you about to, uh—?"

"Yes, Elliot, I am." She pulled open the dress, revealing red satin underwear and an enticing expanse of creamy freckled skin.

His brain went on stun. All he could do was stare— and appreciate. Her bra cupped full breasts so perfectly his hands ached to hold and test their weight, to caress her until she sighed in arousal.

She shrugged and the dress started to slide down, down—

Out here.

In the open.

He bolted forward, a last scrap of sense telling him to shield her gorgeous body. He clasped her shoulders and pulled her to him, stopping the dress from falling away. "Lucy Ann, we're on a balcony. Outside."

A purr rippled up her throat as she wriggled against his throbbing erection. "I know."

Her fragrance beckoned, along with access to silky skin. His mouth watered. That last bit of his sense was going to give up the fight any second.

"We need to go back into our suite."

"I know that, too. So take me inside. Your room or mine. You choose as long as we're together and naked very soon." She leaned into him, her breasts pressing against his chest. "Unless you've changed your mind."

The need to possess tensed all his muscles, the adrenaline rush stronger than coming into a final turn neck and neck.

"Hell, no, I haven't changed my mind. We'll go to my room because there are condoms in my nightstand. And before you ask, yes, I've been wanting and planning to take you to bed again every minute of our journey." He scooped her up into his arms and shouldered the doors open into their suite. The sitting area loomed quiet and empty. "Thank God Mrs. Claymore isn't up looking for a midnight snack."

Her hair trailing loose over his shoulder, Lucy Ann kissed his neck in a series of nibbles up to his ear. "You're supposed to be the race car driver who lives on the edge, and yet you're the one being careful. That's actually quite romantic."

"For you. Always careful for you." Except he hadn't been. He'd left her alone as a teen, gotten her pregnant and stayed away for nearly a year. He refused to let her down again in any way. She deserved better from him.

Lucy Ann deserved the best. Period.

She slid her hand behind his head and brought him closer for a kiss. He took her mouth as fully as he ached to take her body. With every step closer to his bedroom, his body throbbed harder and faster for her. The last few steps to the king-size bed felt like a mile. The massive headboard took up nearly the whole wall, the four posters carved like trees reaching up to the canopy. He was glad now he'd brought her here, a place they'd never been, a fantasy locale for a woman who deserved to be pampered, adored.

Treasured.

He set her on her feet carefully, handling her like spun glass. She tossed the dress aside in a silky flutter of red.

Nibbling her bottom lip and releasing it slowly, seductively, Lucy Ann kicked her high heels off with a flick of each foot. "One of us is *very* overdressed."

"You don't say."

"I do." She hooked her finger in the collar of his shirt and tugged down. Hard. Popping the buttons free in a burst that scattered them along the floor.

Ooooo-kay. So much for spun glass. His libido ramped into high gear. "You seem to be taking charge so nicely I thought you might help me take care of that."

He looked forward to losing more buttons in her deft hands.

"Hmm," she hummed, backing toward the bed until her knees bumped the wooden steps. "If I'm taking charge, then I want you to take off the rest of your clothes while I watch."

"I believe I can comply with that request." Shrugging off his destroyed shirt, he couldn't take his eyes from her as she settled onto the middle of the gold comforter, surrounded by tapestry pillows and a faux-fur throw. He toed off his loafers, his bare feet sinking into the thick Persian rug.

She reclined on the bed, pushing her heels into the mattress to scoot farther up until she could lean against the headboard. "You could have continued your underwear model days and made a mint, you know."

His hands stopped on his belt buckle. "You're killing the mood for me, Lucy Ann. I prefer to forget that brief chapter of my life."

"Briefs?" She giggled at her own pun. "You're right. You're definitely more of a boxers kind of guy now."

Fine, then. She seemed to want to keep this light-hearted, avoiding the heavier subjects they'd touched on while dancing. Now that he thought of it, they'd never gotten around to dinner, either. Which gave him an idea, one he'd be better off starting while he still had his clothes on.

"Stay there, just like that," he said. "I'll be right back."

Belt buckle clanking and loose, he sprinted out to the balcony. He picked up the platter of fruit and cheese and tucked the two plates of flan on top. Balancing the make-shift feast, he padded toward their room, careful not to wake the nanny or Eli.

Backing inside, he elbowed the door closed carefully. Turning, he breathed a sigh of relief to find Lucy Ann waiting. He hadn't really expected her to leave…except for a hint of an instant he'd thought about how quickly she'd run from what they shared last time.

She tipped her head to the side, her honey-streaked brown hair gliding along her shoulder like melted caramel. "You want to eat dinner now?"

He gave her his best bad boy grin. "If you're my plate, then yes, ma'am, I think this is a fine time for us to have supper."

"Okay then. Wouldn't want to mess up our clothes." She tugged off her bra and shimmied out of her panties, her lush curves bared and... Wow.

He almost dropped the damn tray.

Regaining his footing, he set the food on the edge of the bed without once taking his eyes off the long lines of her legs leading up to her caramel curls. He was definitely overdressed for what he had in mind.

He tugged off his slacks along with his boxers. His erection sprang free.

She smiled, her eyes roving over him in an appreciative sweep that made him throb harder. "Elliot?"

"Yes?" He clasped her foot in his hand, lifting it and kissing the inside of her ankle where a delicate chain with a fairy charm surprised him on such a practical woman. What else had he missed about Lucy Ann in the year they'd been apart?

"Do you know what would make this perfect?"

He kissed the inside of her calf. "Name it. I'll make it happen."

"More lights."

He looked up from her leg to her confident eyes reflecting the bedside lamp. "Lights?"

"It's been quite a while since I saw you naked, and last time was rather hurried and with bad lighting."

She was a total and complete turn-on. Everything about her.

"Can do," he said.

He placed her leg back on the bed and turned on the massive cast-iron chandelier full of replica candles that supplemented the glow of the bedside lamp. The rich colors of the bed and the heavy curtains swept back on either side somehow made Lucy Ann seem all the more pale and naked, her creamy flesh as tempting as anything he'd ever seen. The feel of her gaze on him heated his blood to molten lava, his whole body on fire for her.

But no way in hell would he let himself lose control. He took the time to reach for the bedside table, past his vintage copy of *Don Quixote*. Dipping into the drawer, he pulled out a condom. He dropped it on the bed before hitching a knee on the edge and joining her on the mattress. Taking his time, even as urgency thrummed through him, he explored every curve, enjoying the way goose bumps rose along her bared flesh.

She met him stroke for stroke, caress for caress, until he couldn't tell for certain who was mirroring whom. Their hands moved in tandem, their sighs syncing up, until they both breathed faster. He lost track of how long they just enjoyed each other, touching and seeking their fill. At some point, she rolled the condom over him, but he only half registered it since pleasure pulsed through him at her touch—and at the feel of her slick desire on his fingertips as he traced and teased between her legs.

Holding himself in check grew tougher by the second so he angled away, reaching for the platter of food on the corner of the bed.

He pushed the tray along the bed to put it in better reach. Then he plucked a strawberry and placed the plump fruit between his teeth. He slid over her, blanketing her. He throbbed between her legs, nudging, wanting. He leaned closer and pressed the strawberry to her mouth. Her lips parted to close over the plump fruit until they met in a kiss.

She bit into the strawberry and he thrust inside her. The fruity flavor burst over his taste buds at the same time sensation sparked through him. Pleasure. The feel of her clamping around him, holding him deep inside her as a "yes" hissed between her teeth. Her head pressed back into the bolster, her eyes sliding closed.

He moved as her jaw worked, chewing the strawberry. Her head arched back, her throat gliding with a slow swallow. Her breasts pushed upward, beading tight and hard.

Inviting.

Leaning on one elbow, he reached for another berry. He squeezed the fruit in his fist, dribbling the juice over her nipple. She gasped in response. He flicked his tongue over her, tasting her, rolling the beaded tip in his mouth until she moaned for more. The taste of ripe fruit and a hint of something more had him ready to come apart inside her already.

Thrusting over and over, he pushed aside the need to finish, hard and fast. Aching to make this last, for her and for him.

How could he possibly have stayed away from her for so long? For any time at all? How could he have thought for even a second he could be with anyone other than her? They were linked together. They always had been, for as far back as he could remember.

She was his, damn it.

The thought rocketed through him, followed closely by her sighs and moans of completion. Her hands flung out, twisting in the comforter, her teeth sinking deep into her bottom lip as she bit back the cry that might wake others.

Seeing the flush of pleasure wash over her skin

snapped the reins on his restraint and he came, the hot pulse jetting from him into her. Deeper, and yet somehow not deep enough as he already wanted her again.

As his arms gave way and he sank to rest fully on top of her, he could only think, damn straight, she was his.

But he hadn't been able to keep Lucy Ann before. How in the hell was he going to manage to keep the new, more confident woman in his arms?

A woman who didn't need anything from him.

Tingling with anticipation, Lucy Ann angled toward Elliot. "I need another bite now or I am absolutely going to pass out."

She gripped his wrist and guided his spoonful of flan toward her mouth as he chuckled softly. She closed her lips over it and savored the creamy caramel pudding. All of her senses were on hyperalert since she and Elliot had made love—twice. The scent of strawberries still clung to the sheets even though they'd showered together, making love in the large stone spa before coming back to bed.

Eventually, she would have to sleep or she would be a completely ineffective mother. But for now, she wasn't ready to let go of this fantasy night, making love with Elliot in a castle.

The luxurious sheets teased her already-sensitive skin, and she gave herself a moment to soak in the gorgeous surroundings. Beyond Elliot. The man was temptation enough, but he'd brought her to this decadent haven where she could stare up at carvings of a Dionysian revel on the bedposts or lose herself in the images of a colorful, wall-sized tapestry depicting a medieval feast. The figures were almost life-size, gathered around a table, an elegant lord and lady in the middle and an array of characters all around from lecherous knight to teasing serving maid. Even the scent of dried herbs and flowers that emanated from the linens immersed her in a fantasy world.

One she never wanted to end.

She scooped her spoon through the flan and offered a bite to her own sexy knight. "I have to say our dance tonight ended much better than our sophomore homecoming ever could have."

"You're right about that." He dipped his spoon into the dessert for her, picking up the rhythm of feeding each other. "Lady, you are rocking the hell out of that sheet."

He filled her whole fairy-tale fantasy well with his broad shoulders and muscular chest, the sheet wrapped around his waist. There was a timeless quality about this place that she embraced. It kept her from looking into the future. She intended to make the absolute most of this chance to be together.

They'd had sex before. They knew each other's bodies intimately. Yet there was a newness about this moment. She looked different now that she'd had a baby. Her body had changed. *She* had changed in other ways, as well. She had a growing confidence now, personally and professionally.

Lucy Ann searched Elliot's eyes…and found nothing but desire. His gaze stroked over her with appreciation and yes, even possession—stoking the heat still simmering inside her.

"I have to confess something." She angled forward to accept the next bite he fed her.

His face went somber in a flash even as he took the spoonful of flan she brought to his mouth. He swallowed, then said, "Tell me whatever you need to. I'm not going anywhere."

She carefully set her utensil onto the platter by the last strawberry, her body humming with the memory of the moment they'd shared the fruit, the moment he'd thrust inside her. The intensity of it all threatened to overwhelm her. She desperately needed to lighten the moment before they waded into deeper waters.

"I may like simplicity in many parts of my life—" she paused for effect, then stretched out like a lazy cat until the sheet slithered away from her breasts "—but I am totally addicted to expensive linens."

"God, Lucy Ann." He hauled her against his side, her nipples beading tighter at the feel of his bare skin. "You scared the hell out of me with talk of confessions."

"I'm serious as a heart attack here." She rested her cheek on his chest, the warmth of him seeping into her. "Every night when I crawled into bed—and trust me, cheap mattresses also suck a lot more than I remembered—those itchy sheets made me long for Egyptian cotton."

"Ahhh, now I understand." He tugged the comforter over them. "The fairy tale here is *The Princess and the Pea.* I will be very sure you always have the best mattresses and sheets that money can buy." He patted her butt.

"My prince," she said, joking to keep talk of the future light for now, all the while knowing that inevitably they would have to steer the conversation in another direction. "I don't think I ever said congratulations on your win today. I'm sorry you missed out on the parties tonight."

"I'm not sorry at all." He stroked back her hair, extending the length with his fingers and letting damp strands glide free. "This is exactly where I wanted to be. Celebrating with you, without clothes—best party ever."

"You do deserve to celebrate your success though. You've come a long way through sheer determination." She hooked a leg over his, enjoying the way they fit.

"Although I have to say, I've always been surprised you chose Formula One over the NASCAR route, given your early days racing the dirt-track circuit."

Why had she never thought to question him about this before? She'd simply followed, accepting. He'd always taken the lead in life and on the track.

He'd begun racing with adults at fourteen years old, then picked it up again when he graduated from the military high school in North Carolina. He was a poster boy for the reformative success of the school even without people knowing he periodically helped out Interpol.

Elliot rested his chin on her head, his breath warm on her scalp. "I guess I have a confession of my own to make. I wanted to go to college and major in English. But I had to make a living. I went back to racing after school because my credit was shot."

English? It made sense given the way he'd always kept a book close at hand, and yet she couldn't believe he'd never mentioned that dream. A whole new side of Elliot emerged, making her wonder what else he'd kept secret.

"Because of your arrest history?"

His chest rose and fell with a heavy sigh. "Because my father took out credit cards in my name."

Her eyes closing, she hugged an arm tighter around him. "I'm so sorry. Nothing should surprise me when it comes to that man, but it still sucks to hear. I'm just so glad you got away from him."

"You should be mad at me for leaving you," he repeated, his voice hoarse. "I let you down."

"I don't agree." She kissed his chest before continuing. "You did what you needed to. I missed you when they sent you to North Carolina, but I understood."

"All the same, you were still hurt by what I did. I could see that then. I can even feel it now. Tell me the truth."

So much for keeping things light. They would always have to cycle around to the weightier stuff eventually. "I understand why you needed a way out, believe me, I do. I just wish you'd spoken to me, given me an opportunity to weigh in and figure out how we could both leave. That place was bearable with you around. Without you…"

She squeezed her eyes closed, burying her face in his chest, absorbing the vibrant strength of him to ward off the chill seeping into her bones.

"I like to think if I could go back and change the past that I would. Except I did the same thing all over again. I let you go. You deserve to be put first in someone's life, someone who won't let you down."

Where was he going with this? Where did she *want* him to go?

After that, he stayed silent so long she thought for a moment he had drifted off midthought, then his hand started to rove along her spine slowly. Not in a seductive way; more of a touch of connection.

He kissed the top of her head, whispering into her hair still damp from their shared shower, "I didn't want to leave you back in high school. You have to know that." His voice went ragged with emotion. "But I didn't have anything to offer you if we left together. And I couldn't stay any longer. I just couldn't see another way out except to get arrested."

She struggled to sift through his words, to understand what he was trying to tell her. "You stole cars on purpose, hoping the cops would catch you?"

"That pretty much sums it up." His hand slid to rest on her hip, his voice strangely calm in contrast to his racing heart. "After that first night in jail, I started stealing cars on a regular basis. I didn't expect to be so good at it. I thought I would get caught much earlier."

"Why did you want to get caught?" she repeated, needing to understand, wondering how she didn't know this about him. She'd thought they told each other everything.

"I figured jail was safer than home," he said simply. "I didn't worry so much about myself with my dad, but I worried what he would do to the people around me."

"You mean me and your mother?"

He nodded against her head. "Remember when we went on that trip to the beach and my old rebuilt truck broke down?"

"You mean when the tires fell off." Only his incredible reflexes had kept them from crashing into a ditch. It had been a near miss.

"Right. When the first one fell off, I thought what crappy luck. Then the second one came off, too...."

Her stomach lurched at the memory. "We were lucky we didn't get T-boned in traffic. You had fast instincts, even then."

His arms twitched around her, holding her too tightly. "I found out that my father had taken out a life insurance policy on me."

She gasped, rising up on her elbows to look him in the eyes. His expression was completely devoid of emotion, but she could see the horror that must be on her face reflected in his eyes.

"Elliot, do you really believe your father tried to kill you?"

"I'm sure of it," he said with certainty, pushing up to sit, the covers rustling and twisting around their legs.

"You had to have been so scared."

Why hadn't he told her? Although the second she finished that thought, she already knew the answer. He didn't want to put her at risk. Debating the fact now, insisting he should have told the police, seemed moot after so long. Better to just listen and figure out why he was telling her this now.

"I didn't have the money to strike out on my own. I knew the odds of teens on the street." His head fell back against the carved headboard. "I figured the kids in juvie couldn't be as bad as my old man."

"Except you were sent to military reform school instead."

Thank heavens, too, since his life had been turned around because of his time in that school, thanks to his friends and the headmaster. The system did work for the best sometimes. Someone somewhere had seen the good deep inside of Elliot.

"I finally caught a lucky break." He cupped the back of her head, his fingers massaging her scalp. "I'm just so damn sorry I had to leave you behind. I see now I should have figured out another way."

"It all worked out—"

"Did it?" he asked, his eyes haunted. "Your mom's boyfriends... We've talked about so much over the years but we've never discussed that time when I was away."

Slowly, she realized what he was asking, and the thought that he'd worried about her, about that, for all these years... Her heart broke for him and the worries he'd had. She wondered if that's why he'd been so protective, giving her a job, keeping her with him—out of guilt?

"Elliot, the guys my mom saw were jerks, yes, and a few of them even tried to cop a feel, but none of them were violent. Some may have been perverts but they weren't rapists. So I was able to take care of myself by avoiding them. I escaped to Aunt Carla's until things settled down or until Mom and her latest guy broke up."

"You shouldn't have had to handle it yourself, to hide from your own home." Anger and guilt weighted his words and tightened his jaw until the tendons flexed along his neck. "Your mother should have been there for you. *I* should have been there."

She didn't want him to feel guilty or to feel sorry for her. Angling up, she cupped his face in her hands. "I don't want you to feel obligated to be my protector."

"I don't know what else I can be for you." His voice was ragged with emotion, his eyes haunted.

They could have been teenagers again, the two of them clinging to each other because there was so little else for them. So much pain. So much betrayal by parents who should have valued them and kept them safe. Her shared past with Elliot wrapped around her so tightly she felt bound to him in a way she couldn't find words to explain but felt compelled to express, even if only physically.

Soaking in the feel of bare flesh meeting flesh, Lucy Ann kissed Elliot, fully, deeply. She savored the taste of flan and strawberries and *him*. A far more intoxicating combination than any alcohol.

And he was all hers, for tonight.

Nine

Their tongues met and tangled as Lucy Ann angled her mouth over Elliot's. They fit so seamlessly together as she tried to give him some sort of comfort, even if only in the form of distraction. Sex didn't solve problems, but it sure made the delaying a hell of a lot more pleasurable. Her mind filled with the sensation of him, the scents of them together.

His hands banded around her waist, and he urged her over him. She swung her leg over his lap, straddling him. His arousal pressed between her legs, nudging against the tight bundle of nerves at her core.

She writhed against him, her body on fire for him. "I need… I want…"

"Tell me, Lucy Ann," he said between kisses and nips, tasting along her neck, "tell me what you want."

She didn't even know what would settle out their lives or how to untangle the mess they'd made of their world.

Not to mention their emotions. "Right now, I just need you inside me."

"That's not what I meant." He held her with those mesmerizing green eyes, familiar eyes that had been a part of her life for as long as she could remember.

"Shh, don't ruin this." She pressed two fingers to his lips. She didn't want to risk their conversation leading down a dangerous path as it had eleven months ago.

Even thinking about their fight chilled her. That argument had led to the most painful time in her life, the time without the best friend she'd ever had. They couldn't go that route again. They had Eli to consider.

And as for their own feelings?

She shied away from those thoughts, determined to live in the moment. She shifted to reach in the bedside table drawer for another condom. He plucked it from between her fingers and sheathed himself quickly, efficiently, before positioning her over him again. Slowly, carefully—blissfully—she lowered herself onto him, taking the length of him inside her until he touched just... the right...spot.

Yessss.

Her eyelids grew heavy but the way he searched her face compelled her to keep her eyes open, to stare back at him as she rolled her hips to meet his thrusts. Every stroke sent ripples of pleasure tingling through her as they synced up into a perfect rhythm. Her palms flattened against his chest, her fingers digging into the bunched muscles twitching under her touch. A purr of feminine satisfaction whispered free as she reveled in the fact that she made him feel every bit as out of control as he made her feel.

His hands dug into her hips then eased, caressing up her sides then forward to cup her breasts. She sighed at the gentle rasp of his callused fingers touching her so instinctively, his thumbs gliding over nipples until she feared she would come apart now. Too soon. She ached for this to last, to hang on to the blissful forgetfulness they could find in each other's arms. She flowed forward to cover him, moving slower, holding back.

Elliot's arms slid around her, and he drew her earlobe between his teeth. Just an earlobe. Yet her whole body tensed up with that final bit of sensation that sent her hurtling into fulfillment. Her nails dug into his shoulders, and she cried out as her release crested.

He rolled her over, and she pushed back, tumbling them again until the silver tray went crashing to the floor, the twang of pewter plates clanking. He kissed her hard, taking her cries of completion into his mouth. As orgasm gripped her again and again, his arms twitched around her, his body pulsing, his groans mingling with hers until she melted in the aftermath.

Panting, she lay beside him, her leg hitched over his hip, an arm draped over him. Her whole body was limp from exhaustion. She barely registered him pulling the comforter over her again.

Maybe they could make this friendship work, friendship combined with amazing sex. Being apart hadn't made either of them happy.

Could this be enough? Friendship and sex? Could they learn to trust each other again as they once had?

They had the rest of the month together to figure out the details. If only they could have sex until they couldn't think about the future.

His breath settled into an even pattern with a soft snore. What a time to realize she'd never slept with him before. She'd seen him nap plenty of times, falling asleep with a book on his chest, but never once had she stayed through the night with him.

For now, it was best she keep it that way. No matter how tempted she was to indulge herself, she wouldn't make the mistakes of her past again. Not with Eli to think about.

Careful not to wake her generous, sexy lover, she eased from the bed, tiptoeing around the scattered cutlery and dishes that looked a lot like the disjointed parts of her life. Beautiful pieces, but such a jumbled mess there was no way to put everything back together.

"Lucy Ann?" Elliot called in a groggy voice. He reached out for her. "Come back to bed."

She pulled on her red wraparound dress and tied it quickly before gathering her underwear. "I need to go to Eli. I'll see you in the morning."

Her bra and panties in her hand, she raced from his room and tried to convince herself she wasn't making an even bigger mess of her life by running like a coward.

"Welcome to Monte Carlo, Eli," Elliot said to his son, carrying the baby in the crook of his arm, walking the floor with his cranky child while everyone else slept. He'd heard Eli squawk and managed to scoop him up before Lucy Ann woke.

But then she was sprawled out on her bed, looking dead to the world after their trip to Monte Carlo—with a colicky kid.

The day had been so busy with travel, he hadn't had a chance to speak to Lucy Ann alone. But then she hadn't gone out of her way to make that possible, either. If he hadn't known better, he would have thought she was hiding from him.

Only there was no reason for her to do so. The sex

last night had been awesome. They hadn't argued. Hell, he didn't know what was wrong, but her silence today couldn't be missed.

Compounding matters, Eli had become progressively irritable as the day passed. By the time his private plane had landed in Monte Carlo, Elliot was ready to call a doctor. Lucy Ann and the nanny had both reassured him that Eli was simply suffering from gas and exhaustion over having his routine disrupted.

Of course that only proved Lucy Ann's point that a child shouldn't be living on the road, but damn it all, Elliot wasn't ready to admit defeat. Especially not after last night. He and Lucy Ann were so close to connecting again.

He'd hoped Monte Carlo would go a long way toward scoring points in his campaign. He owned a place here. A home with friends who lived in the area. Sure it was a condominium and his friend owned a casino. But his friend was a dad already. And the flat was spacious, with a large garden terrace. He would have to add some kind of safety feature to the railing before Eli became mobile. He scanned the bachelor pad with new eyes and he saw a million details in a different light. Rather than fat leather sofas and heavy wooden antiques, he saw sharp edges and climbing hazards.

"What do you think, Eli?" he asked his son, staring down into the tiny features all scrunched up and angry. "Are you feeling any better? I'm thinking it may be time for you to eat, but I hate to wake your mama. What do you say I get you one of those bottles with expressed milk?"

Eli blinked back up at him with wide eyes, his fists and feet pumping.

He'd always thought babies all looked the same, like

tiny old men. Except now he knew he could pick out Eli from dozens of other babies in a heartbeat.

How strange to see parts of himself and Lucy Ann mixed together in that tiny face. Yet the longer he looked, the more that mixture became just Eli. The kid had only been in his life for a week. Yet now there didn't seem to be a pre-Eli time. Any thoughts prior to seeing him were now colored by the presence of him. As if he had somehow already existed on some plane just waiting to make an appearance.

Eli's face scrunched up tighter in that sign he was about to scream bloody murder. Elliot tucked his son against his shoulder and patted his back while walking to the fridge to get one of the bottles he'd seen Lucy Ann store there.

He pulled it out, started to give it to his son...then remembered something about cold bottles not being good. He hadn't paid a lot of attention when his friends took care of baby stuff, but something must have permeated his brain. Enough so that he tugged his cell phone from his pocket and thumbed speed dial for his buddy Conrad Hughes. He always stayed up late. Conrad had said once that life as a casino magnate had permanently adjusted his internal clock.

The phone rang only once. "This is Hughes. Speak to me, Elliot."

"I need advice."

"Sure, financial? Work? Name it."

"Um, babies." He stared at the baby and the bottle on the marble slab counter. Life had definitely changed. "Maybe you should put Jayne on the line."

"I'm insulted," Conrad joked, casino bells and music drifting over the airwaves. "Ask your question. Besides, Jayne's asleep. Worn out from the kiddo."

"The nanny's sick and Lucy Ann really needs to sleep in." He swayed from side to side. "She's been trying to keep up with her work, the baby, the traveling."

"And your question?"

"Oh, right. I forgot. Sleep deprivation's kicking in, I think," he admitted, not that he would say a word to Lucy Ann after the way she was freaking out over him having a wreck.

"Happens to the best of us, brother. You were just the last man to fall."

"Back to my question. When I give the baby a bottle of this breast milk from the refrigerator, do I heat it in the microwave? And I swear if you laugh, I'm going to kick your ass later."

"I'm only laughing on the inside. Never out loud." Conrad didn't have to laugh. Amusement drenched his words.

"I can live with that." As long as he got the advice.

"Run warm water over the bottle. No microwave. Do not heat it in water on the stove," Conrad rattled off like a pro. "If he doesn't eat it all, pour it out. You can't save and reuse it. Oh, and shake it up."

"You're too good at this," Elliot couldn't resist saying as he turned on the faucet.

"Practice."

"This has to be the strangest conversation of my life." He played his fingers through the water to test the temperature and found it was warming quickly. He tucked the bottled milk underneath the spewing faucet with one hand, still holding his son to his shoulder with the other.

"It'll be commonplace before you know it."

Would it? "I hope so."

The sound of casino bells softened, as if Conrad had

gone into another room. "What about you and Lucy Ann?"

Elliot weighed his answer carefully before saying simply, "We're together."

"Together-together?" Conrad asked.

Elliot glanced through the living area at the closed bedroom door and the baby in his arms. "I'm working on it."

"You've fallen for her." His friend made it more of a statement than a question.

So why couldn't he bring himself to simply agree? "Lucy Ann and I have been best friends all our lives. We have chemistry."

Best friends. His brothers all called themselves best friends, but now he realized he'd never quite paired up with a best bud the way they all had. He was a part of the group. But Lucy Ann was his best friend, always had been.

"You'd better come up with a smoother answer than that if you ever get around to proposing to her. Women expect more than 'you're a great friend and we're super together in the sack.'"

Proposing? The word *marriage* hadn't crossed his mind, and he realized now that it should have. He should have led with that from the start. He should have been an honorable, stand-up kind of guy and offered her a ring rather than a month-long sex fest.

"I'm not that much of an idiot."

He hoped.

"So you are thinking about proposing."

He was now. The notion fit neatly in his brain, like the missing piece to a puzzle he'd been trying to complete since Lucy Ann left a year ago.

"I want my son to have a family, and I want Lucy Ann to be happy." He turned off the water and felt the bottle. Seemed warm. He shook it as instructed. "I'm just not sure I know how to make that happen. Not many long-term role models for happily ever after on my family tree."

"Marriage is work, no question." Conrad whistled softly on a long exhale. "I screwed up my own pretty bad once, so maybe I'm not the right guy to ask for advice."

Conrad and Jayne had been separated for three years before reuniting.

"But you fixed your marriage. So you're probably the best person to ask." Elliot was getting into this whole mentor notion. Why hadn't he thought to seek out some help before? He took his son and the bottle back into the living room of his bachelor pad, now strewn with baby gear. "How do you make it right when you've messed up this bad? When you've let so much time pass?"

"Grovel," Conrad said simply.

"That's it?" Elliot asked incredulously, dropping into his favorite recliner. He settled his son in the crook of his arm and tucked the bottle in his mouth. "That's your advice? Grovel?"

"It's not just a word. You owe her for being a jackass this past year. Like I said before. Relationships are work, man. Hard work. Tougher than any Interpol assignment old headmaster Colonel Salvatore could ever give us. But the payoff is huge if you can get it right."

"I hope so."

"Hey, I gotta go. Text just came in. Kid's awake and Jayne doesn't believe in nighttime nannies. So we're in the walking dead stage of parenthood right now." He didn't sound at all unhappy about it. "Don't forget. Shake the milk and burp the kid if you want to keep your suit clean."

Shake. Burp. Grovel. "I won't forget."

Lucy Ann blinked at the morning sun piercing the slight part in her curtains. She'd slept in this room in Elliot's posh Monte Carlo digs more times than she could remember. He'd even had her choose her own decor since they spent a lot of off-season time here, too.

She'd chosen an über-feminine French toile in pinks and raspberries, complete with an ornate white bed— Renaissance antiques. And the best of the best mattresses. She stretched, luxuriating in the well-rested feeling, undoubtedly a by-product of the awesome bed and even more incredible sex. She couldn't remember how long it had been since she'd woken up refreshed rather than dragging, exhausted. Certainly not since Eli had been born—

Blinking, she took in the morning sun, then gasped. "Eli!"

She jumped from the bed and raced over to the portable crib Elliot had ordered set up in advance. Had her baby slept through the night? She looked in the crib and found it empty. Her heart lurched up to her throat.

Her bare feet slipping on the hardwood floor, she raced out to the living room and stopped short. Elliot sat in his favorite recliner, holding their son. He looked so at ease with the baby cradled in the crook of his arm. An empty bottle sat on the table beside them.

Elliot toyed with his son's foot. "I have plans for you, little man. There are so many books to read. *Gulliver's Travels* and *Lord of the Rings* were favorites of mine as a kid. And we'll play with Matchbox cars when you're older. Or maybe you'll like trains or airplanes? Your choice."

Relaxing, Lucy Ann sagged against the door frame in relief. "You're gender stereotyping our child."

Glancing up, Elliot smiled at her, so handsome with a five o'clock shadow peppering his jaw and baby spit-up dotting his shoulder it was all she could do not to kiss him.

"Good morning, beautiful," he said, his eyes sliding over her silky nightshirt with an appreciation that all but mentally pulled the gown right off her. "Eli can be a chef or whatever he wants, as long as he's happy."

"Glad to hear you say that." She padded barefoot across the room and sat on the massive tapestry otto-man between the sofa and chairs. "I can't believe I slept in so late this morning."

"Eli and I managed just fine. And if I ran into problems, I had plenty of backup."

"I concede you chose well with the nanny." She wasn't used to taking help with Eli, but she could get addicted to this kind of assistance quickly. "Mrs. Clayworth's amazing and a great help without being intrusive."

"You're not upset that I didn't wake you?"

She swept her tangled hair back over her shoulders. "I can't think any mother of an infant would be upset over an extra two hours of sleep."

"Glad you're happy, Sleeping Beauty." His heated gaze slid over the satin clinging to her breasts.

"Ah, your fairy-tale romancing theme."

He arched an eyebrow. "You catch on fast. If you were to stay with me for the whole racing season, we could play Aladdin and his lamp."

His talk of the future made her…uncomfortable. She was just getting used to the shift in their relationship, adding a sexual level on a day-to-day basis. So she ignored the part about staying longer and focused on the fairy tale. "You've been fantasizing about me as a belly dancer?"

"Now that you mention it…"

"Lucky for us both, I'm rested and ready." She curled her toes into the hand-knotted silk Persian rug that would one day be littered with toys. "You're going to be a wonderful father."

As the words fell from her mouth she knew them to be true, not a doubt in her mind. And somehow she'd slid into talking about the future anyway.

"Well, I sure as hell learned a lot from my father about how not to be a dad." His gaze fell away from her and back to their child. "And the things I didn't learn, I intend to find out, even if that means taking a class or reading every parenting book on the shelves since I never had much of a role model."

Clearly, he was worried about this. She leaned forward to touch his knee. "Does that mean I'm doomed to be a crummy mother?"

"Of course not." He covered her hand with his. "Okay, I see your point. And thanks for the vote of confidence."

"For what it's worth, I do think you've had a very good role model." She linked fingers with him. "The colonel. Your old headmaster has been there for you, the way my aunt has for me. Doing the best they could within a flawed system that sent them broken children to fix."

"I don't like to think of myself as broken." His jaw clenched.

"It's okay, you know—" she rubbed his knee "—to be sad or angry about the past."

"It's a lot easier to just speed around the track, even smash into walls, rather than rage at the world." His throat moved with a long swallow.

"I'm not so sure I like that coping mechanism. I would

be so sad if anything happened to you." And wasn't that the understatement of the year? She had to admit, though, she'd been worrying more about him lately, fearing the distractions she brought to his life, also fearing he might have beat the odds one time too many.

He squeezed her hand, his eyes as serious as she'd ever seen them. "I would quit racing. For you."

"And I would never ask you to do that. Not for me."

"So you would ask for Eli?"

She churned his question around in her mind, unable to come up with an answer that didn't involve a lengthy discussion of the future.

"I think this is entirely too serious a conversation before I've had breakfast."

Scooping up her son from Elliot's arms, she made tracks for the kitchen, unable to deny the truth. Even though she stayed in the condo, she was running from him now every bit as much as she'd run eleven months ago.

Ten

Steering through the narrow streets of Monte Carlo, Elliot drove his new Mercedes S65 AMG along the cliff road leading to the Hughes mansion. His Maserati wouldn't hold a baby seat, so he'd needed a sedan that combined space and safety with his love of finely tuned automobiles. He felt downright domesticated driving Lucy Ann and their son to a lunch with friends. She was meeting with Jayne Hughes and Jayne's baby girl while he went over to the track.

Last time he'd traveled this winding road, he'd been driving Jayne and Conrad to the hospital—Conrad had been too much of a mess to climb behind the wheel of his SUV. Jayne had been in labor. She'd delivered their baby girl seventeen minutes after they'd arrived at the hospital.

How strange to think he knew more about his friend's first kid coming into the world than he knew about the birth of his own son.

His fingers clenched around the steering wheel as they wound up a cliff-side road overlooking the sea. "Tell me about the day Eli was born."

"Are you asking me because you're angry or because you want to know?"

A good question. It wouldn't help to say both probably came into play, so he opted for, "I will always regret that I wasn't there when he came into this world, that I missed out on those first days of his life. But I understand that if we're going to move forward here, I can't let that eat at me. We both are going to have to give a little here. So the answer to your question is, I want to know because I'm curious about all things relating to Eli."

She touched his knee lightly. "Thank you for being honest."

"That's the only way we're going to get through this, don't you think?"

He glanced over at her quickly, taking in the beautiful lines of her face with the sunlight streaming through the window.

Why had it taken him so long to notice?

"Okay…" She inhaled a shaky breath. "I had an appointment the week of my due date. I really expected to go longer since so many first-time moms go overdue. But the doctor was concerned about Eli's heart rate. He did an ultrasound and saw the placenta was separating from the uterine wall— Am I getting too gross for you here?"

"Keep talking," he commanded, hating that he hadn't been there to make things easier, less frightening for her. If he hadn't been so pigheaded, he would have been there to protect her. Assure her.

"The doctor scheduled me for an immediate cesarean section. I didn't even get to go home for my toothbrush," she joked in an attempt to lighten the mood.

He wasn't laughing. "That had to be scary for you. I wish I could have been with you. We helped each other through a lot of tough times over the years."

"I did try to call you," she confessed softly, "right before I went in. But your phone went straight to voice mail. I tried after, too…I assumed you were off on an Interpol secret 'walkabout' for Colonel Salvatore."

"I was." He'd done the math in his head. Knew the case he'd been working at the time.

"I know I could have pushed harder and found you." She shook her head regretfully. "I didn't even leave a message. I'm so sorry for that. You may be able to move past it, but I'm not sure I'll ever forgive myself."

He stayed silent, not sure what to say to make this right for both of them.

"What would we have done if Malcolm and Conrad hadn't kidnapped you from the bachelor party?"

Damn good question. "I like to think I would have come to my senses and checked on you. I don't know how the hell I let eleven months pass."

"Or how you found a fiancée so fast," she blurted out. "You proposed to another woman barely three months after we slept together. Yes, that's a problem for me."

He weighed his words carefully. "This may sound strange, but Gianna was the one who got shortchanged. I obviously didn't care about her the way I should have. I wasn't fair to her."

Her smile was tight. "Excuse me if I'm not overly concerned about being fair to Gianna. And from what I read in the news, she broke things off with you. Not the other way around. If she hadn't left, would you have married her?"

Stunned, he downshifted around a corner. She'd read about his breakup? She'd left, but kept tabs on him. If only he'd done the same with her, he would have known about Eli. As much as Elliot wanted to blame a remote Interpol stint for keeping him out of touch, he knew he should have followed up with Lucy Ann.

Then why hadn't he? She'd been so good to him, always there for him, always forgiving him. Damn it, he didn't deserve her— Could that have been part of why he'd stayed away? Out of guilt for taking so much from her all their lives?

That she could think he still wanted Gianna, especially after what he and Lucy Ann had just shared… Incomprehensible.

"No. I didn't want to marry her. We broke off the engagement. I knew it was inevitable. She just spoke first."

She nodded tightly. "Fine, I appreciate your honesty. I'm still not totally okay with the fact that you raced right back to her after we… Well, I'm just not okay with it. But I'm working on it."

Conrad had told him to grovel. Elliot scrounged inside himself for a way to give her what she needed.

"Fair enough. At least I know where I stand with you." He stared at the road ahead, struggling. Groveling was tougher than he'd expected after the way his father had beaten him to his knees so many times. "That was the hardest part about growing up with my old man. The uncertainty. I'm not saying it would have been okay if he'd punched me on a regular basis. But the sick feeling in my gut as I tried to gauge his moods? That was a crappy way to live."

"I'm so sorry." Her hand fell to rest on his knee again. This time she didn't pull away.

"I know. You saved my sanity back then." He placed his hand over hers. "I always knew it was you who let the air out of my dad's tires that time in sixth grade."

She sat upright. "How did you know?"

"Because you did it while I was away on that science fair trip. So I couldn't be blamed or catch the brunt of his anger." He rubbed her hand along the spot on her finger where he should have put a ring already. "Do I have the details correct?"

"That was the idea. Couldn't have your father get away with everything."

"He didn't. Not in the end." There'd never been a chance to make peace with his bastard of an old man—never a chance to confront him, either.

"I guess there's a sad sort of poetic justice that he died in a bar fight while you were off at reform school."

Her words surprised him. "You're a bloodthirsty one."

"When it comes to protecting the people in my life? Absolutely."

She was freaking amazing. He couldn't deny the rush of admiration for the woman she'd become—that she'd always been, just hidden under the weight of her own problems.

And on the heels of that thought, more guilt piled on top of him for all the ways he'd let her down. Damn it all, he had to figure out how to make this right with her. He had to pull out all the stops as Conrad advised.

Full throttle.

He had to win her over to be his wife.

Lucy Ann sat on the terrace with Jayne Hughes, wondering how a woman who'd been separated for three years could now be such a happily contented wife and new mother. What was her secret? How had they overcome the odds?

There was no denying the peaceful air that radiated off the bombshell blonde with her baby girl cradled in a sling. The Hughes family split their time between their home in Monte Carlo and a home in Africa, where Jayne worked as a nurse at a free clinic her husband funded along with another Alpha Brother. She made it all look effortless whether she was serving up luncheon on fine china or cracking open a boxed lunch under a sprawling shea butter tree.

Lucy Ann patted her colicky son on his precious little back. He seemed to have settled to sleep draped over her knees, which wasn't particularly comfortable, but she wasn't budging an inch as long as he was happy.

Jayne paused in her lengthy ramble about the latest addition to the pediatrics wing at the clinic to tug something from under the plate of petits fours. "Oh, I almost forgot to give you this pamphlet for Elliot."

"For Elliot?" She took it from Jayne, the woman's short nails hinting at her more practical side. "On breast-feeding?"

"He called Conrad with questions the other night." She adjusted her daughter to the other breast in such a smooth transition the cloth baby sling covered all. "I don't know why he didn't just look it up on Google. Anyhow, this should tell him everything he needs to know."

"Thank you." She tucked the pamphlet in her purse, careful not to disturb her son. "He didn't tell me he called your husband for help."

"He was probably too embarrassed. Men can be proud that way." She sipped her ice water, sun glinting off the Waterford crystal that Lucy Ann recalled choosing for a wedding gift to the couple.

There'd been a time when tasks like that—picking out expensive trinkets for Elliot's wealthy friends—had made her nervous. As if the wrong crystal pattern could call her out as an interloper in Elliot Starc's elegant world.

But it had taken walking away from the glitz and glamour to help her see it for what it really was...superficial trappings that didn't mean a lot in the long run. Lucy Ann was far more impressed with Jayne's nursing capabilities and her motherhood savvy than with what kind of place setting graced her table.

"There's a lot to learn about parenting," Lucy Ann acknowledged. "Especially for someone who didn't grow up around other kids." She would have been overwhelmed without Aunt Carla's help.

And wasn't it funny to think that, even though she'd traveled the globe with Elliot for a decade, she'd still learned the most important things back home in South Carolina?

"I think it's wonderful that he's trying. A lot of men would just dump all the tough stuff onto a nanny." Jayne shot a glance over her shoulder through the open balcony doors, somehow knowing Conrad had arrived without even looking.

"I just suggested that it wouldn't hurt to let someone else change the diapers," said Mr. Tall, Dark and Brooding. "Who the hell wants to change a diaper? That doesn't make me a bad human being."

Lucy Ann had to admit, "He has a point."

Jayne set her glass down. "Don't encourage him."

Conrad chuckled as he reached for his daughter. "Lucy Ann, let me know when you're done. I promised Elliot I would drive you and the kidlet back to the condo. He said he's running late at the track. Have fun, ladies. The princess and I are going to read the *Wall Street Journal*."

Conrad disappeared back into the house with his daughter, words about stocks and short sales carrying on the wind spoken in a singsong tone as if telling her a nursery rhyme.

Lucy Ann leaned back in the chair and turned her water glass on the table, watching the sunlight refracting prisms off the cut crystal. "I envy your tight-knit support group. Elliot and I didn't have a lot of friends when we were growing up. He was the kid always in trouble so parents didn't invite him over. And I was too shy to make friends."

"You're not shy anymore," Jayne pointed out.

"Not that I let people see."

"We've known you for years. I would hope you could consider us your friends, too."

They'd known each other, but she'd been Elliot's employee. It wasn't that his friends had deliberately excluded her, but Conrad had been separated for years, and only recently had the rest of them started marrying. She knew it would be easier for all of them if she made the effort here.

"We'll certainly cross paths because of Eli," Lucy Ann said simply.

"And Elliot?"

The conversation was starting to get too personal for her comfort. "We're still working on that."

"But you're making progress."

"Have you been reading the tabloids?"

"I don't bother with those." Jayne waved dismissively. "I saw the way you two looked at each other when Elliot dropped you off."

In spite of herself, Lucy Ann found herself aching to talk to someone after all, and Jayne seemed the best candidate. "He's into the thrill of the chase right now. Things will go back to normal eventually."

"I'm not so sure I agree. He seems different to me." Jayne's pensive look faded into a grin. "They all have to grow up and settle down sometime."

"What about—" She didn't feel comfortable discussing the guys' Interpol work out in the open, so she simply said, "Working with the colonel after graduation and following a call to right bigger wrongs? How do they give that up to be regular family guys?"

"Good question." Jayne pinched the silver tongs to shuffle a petit four and fruit onto a dessert plate. "Some still take an active part once they're married, but once the children start coming, things do change. They shift to pulling the strings. They become more like Salvatore."

"Mine is a bit wilder than yours." When had she started thinking of Elliot as *hers*? Although on some level he'd been hers since they were children. "I mean, seriously, he crashes cars into walls for a living."

"You've known that about him from the start. So why are things different now?"

"I don't know how to reconcile our friendship with everything else that's happened." The whole "friends with benefits" thing was easier said than done.

"By 'everything else' you mean the smoking hot sex, of course." Jayne grinned impishly before popping a grape in her mouth.

"I had forgotten how outspoken you can be."

"Comes with the territory of loving men like these. They don't always perceive subtleties."

True enough. Lucy Ann speared a chocolate strawberry and willed herself not to blush at the heated memories the fruit evoked. "Outspoken or not, I'm still no closer to an answer."

Jayne nudged the gold-rimmed china plate aside and leaned her arms on the table. "You don't have to reconcile the two ways of being. It's already done—or it will be once you stop fighting."

Could Jayne be right? Maybe the time had come to

truly give him a chance. To see if he was right. To see if they could really have a fairy-tale life together.

Fear knotted her gut, but Lucy Ann wasn't the shy little girl anymore. She was a confident woman and she was all-in.

Elliot shrugged out of his black leather jacket with a wince as he stepped into the dark apartment. He'd done his prelim runs as always, checklists complete, car scrutinized to the last detail, and yet somehow he'd damn near wiped out on a practice run.

Every muscle in his body ached from reactionary tensing. Thank goodness Lucy Ann hadn't been there as she would have been in the past as his assistant. He didn't want her worrying. He didn't want to risk a confrontation.

He tossed the jacket over his arm, walking carefully so he wouldn't wake anyone up. His foot hooked on something in the dark. He bit back a curse and looked down to find…a book? He reached to pick up an ornately bound copy of *Hansel and Gretel*. He started to stand up again and looked ahead to find a trail of books, all leading toward his bedroom. He picked up one book after the other, each a different fairy tale, until he pushed open his door.

His room was empty.

Frowning, he scanned the space and… "Aha…"

More books led to the bathroom, and now that he listened, he could hear the shower running. He set the stack on the chest of drawers and gathered up the last few "crumbs" on his trail, a copy of *Rapunzel* and a Victorian version of *Rumpelstiltskin*. Pushing his way slowly into the bathroom, he smiled at the shadowy outline behind the foggy glass wall. The multiple showerheads shot spray over Lucy Ann as she hummed. She didn't seem to notice he'd arrived.

He peeled off his clothes without making a sound and padded barefoot into the slate-tiled space. He opened the door and stepped into the steam. Lucy Ann stopped singing, but she didn't turn around. The only acknowledgment she gave to his arrival was a hand reaching for him. He linked fingers with her and stepped under the warm jets. The heat melted away the stress from his muscles, allowing a new tension to take hold. He saw the condom packet in the soap dish and realized just how thoroughly she'd thought this through.

He pressed against her back, wrapping his arms around her. Already, his erection throbbed hard and ready, pressed between them.

He sipped water from just behind her ear. "I'm trying to think of what fairy tale you're fantasizing about, and for water, I can only come up with the *Frog Prince.*"

Angling her head to give him better access to her neck, she combed her fingers over his damp hair. "We're writing our own fantasy tonight."

Growling his approval, he slicked his hands over her, taking in the feel of her breasts peaking against his palms. His blood fired hotter through his veins than the water sluicing over them. He slipped a hand between her thighs, stroking satin, finding that sweet bundle of nerves. Banding his arm tighter around her waist, he continued to circle and tease, feeling her arousal lubricate his touch. She sagged back against him, her legs parting to give him easier access.

With her bottom nestled against him, he held on to control by a thread. Each roll of her hips as she milked the most from her pleasure threatened to send him over the edge. But he held back his own release, giving her hers. He tucked two fingers inside her, his thumb still working along that pebbled tightness.

Her sighs and purrs filled the cubicle, the jasmine scent of her riding the steam. Every sound of her impending arousal shot a bolt of pleasure through him, his blood pounding thicker through his veins. Until, yes, she cried out, coming apart in his arms. Her fingernails dug deep into his thighs, cutting half-moons into his flesh as she arched into her orgasm.

He savored every shiver of bliss rippling her body until he couldn't wait any longer. He took the condom from the soap tray and sheathed himself. He pressed her against the shower stall wall, her palms flattened to the stone. Standing behind her, he nudged her legs apart and angled until… He slid home, deep inside her, clamped by damp silken walls as hot and moist as the shower.

Sensation engulfed him, threatened to shake the ground under him as he pushed inside her again and again. Things moved so damn fast… He was so close… Then he heard the sound of her unraveling in his arms. The echoes of her release sent him over the edge. Ecstasy rocked his balance. He flattened a hand against the warm wall to keep from falling over as his completion pulsed until his heartbeat pounded in his ears. Shifting, he pulled out of her, keeping one arm around her.

Slowly, his world expanded beyond just the two of them, and he became aware of the water sheeting over them. The patter of droplets hitting the door and floor.

Tucking her close again, he thought about his near miss at the track today and all the relationship advice from his friends. He'd waited too long these past eleven months to make sure she stayed with him. Permanently. He wouldn't let another minute pass without moving forward with their lives.

He nuzzled her ear. "What kind of house do you want?"

"House?" she asked, her knees buckling.

He steadied her. "I want to build a real house for us, Lucy Ann. Not just condos or rented places here and there."

"Umm…" She licked her lips. The beads on her temple mingled perspiration with water. "What city would you choose?"

He had penthouse suites around the world, but nowhere he stayed long enough to call home. And none of them had the room for a boy to run and play.

"I need a home. We need a home for our son."

"You keep assuming we'll stay together."

Already his proposal was going astray. Could be because most of the blood in his brain was surging south. "Where do you want to live? I'll build two houses next door if that's the way you want it." Living near each other would give him more time to win her over, because he was fast realizing he couldn't give her up. "I have connections with a friend who restores historic homes."

She turned in his arms, pressing her fingers to his lips. "Can we just keep making love instead?"

Banding her wrist in his hand, he kissed it, determined not to let this chance slip away, not to let *her* slip away again. "Let's get married."

She leaned into him, whispering against his mouth as she stroked down between them, molding her palm to the shape of him. "You may have missed the memo…" She caressed up and down, again and again. "But you don't have to propose to get me to sleep with you."

He angled away, staring straight in her eyes, her eyelashes spiky wet. "I'm not joking, so I would appreciate it if you took my proposal seriously."

"Really? Now?" She stepped back, the water showering between them. "You mean this. For Eli, of course."

"Of course Eli factors into the equation." He studied her carefully blank expression. "But it's also because you and I fit as a couple on so many levels. We've been friends forever, and our chemistry… Well, that speaks for itself. We just have to figure out how not to fight afterward and we'll have forever locked and loaded."

The more he talked, the more it felt right.

"Forever?" Her knees folded, and she sat on the stone seat in the corner, her hair dripping water. "Do you think that's even possible for people like you and me?"

"Why shouldn't it be?" He knelt in front of her.

"Because of our pasts." She stroked over his wet hair, cupping his neck, her eyes so bittersweet they tore him to bits. "Our parents. Our own histories. I refuse to spend the rest of my life wondering when the next Gianna is going to walk through the door."

Gianna? He hadn't even thought of her other than when Lucy Ann mentioned her. But looking back, he realized how bad his engagement would have looked to her, how that must have played a role in her keeping quiet about the pregnancy.

This was likely where the groveling came in. "I'm sorry."

"For which part? The engagement? Or the fact you didn't contact me— Hell, forget I said that." She leaned forward to kiss him.

If they kissed, the discussion would be over, opportunity missed. He scooped her up in his arms and pivoted, settling her into his lap as he sat on the stone seat in the corner.

She squawked in protest but he pressed on. "You expected me to follow you? Even after you said—and I quote—'I don't ever want to lay eyes on your irresponsible ass ever again'?"

"And you've never said anything in the heat of the moment that you regretted later?"

Groveling was all well and good, but he wasn't taking the full blame for what shook down these past months. "If you regretted those words, it sure would have been helpful if you'd let me know."

"This is my whole point. We're both so proud, neither one of us could take the steps needed to repair the damage we did. Yes, I am admitting that we both were hurt. Even though you seemed to recover fast with Gianna—" she gave him that tight smile again "—I acknowledge that losing our friendship hurt, as well. But friendship isn't enough to build a marriage on. So can we please go back to the friends-with-benefits arrangement?"

"Damn it, Lucy Ann—"

She traced his face with her fingers. "Do you know what I think?" She didn't wait for him to answer. "I think you don't believe in fairy tales after all. The dates, the romance... It has actually been a game for you after all. A challenge, a competition. Something to win. Not Cinderella or Sleeping Beauty."

"I suspect I've been led into a trap." He'd thought he'd been following all the right signs and taking the steps to fix this, but he'd only seemed to dig a bigger hole for himself.

"Well, you followed my bread crumbs." Her joke fell flat between them, her eyes so much sadder than he'd ever dreamed he could make them.

"So you're sure you don't want to marry me?"

She hesitated, her pulse leaping in her neck. "I'm sure I don't want you to propose to me."

Her rejection stunned him. Somehow he'd expected her to say yes. He'd thought... Hell, he'd taken her for granted all over again and he didn't know how to fix this. Not now. He needed time to regroup. "If I agree to stop pressing for marriage, can we keep having incredible sex with each other?"

"'Til the end of the month."

"Sex for a few weeks? You're okay with sleeping together with an exit strategy already in place?"

"That's my offer." She slid from his lap, stepping back. Away. Putting distance between them on more than just one level. "Take it or leave it."

"Lucy Ann, I'm happy as hell to take you again and again until we're both too exhausted to argue." Although right now, he couldn't deny it. He wanted more from her. "But eventually we're going to have to talk."

Eleven

Lucy sprawled on top of Elliot in bed, satiated, groggy and almost dry from their shower, but not ready for their evening together to end. Elliot seemed content to let the proposal discussion go—for tonight. So this could well be the last uncomplicated chance she had to be with him.

The ceiling fan *click, click, clicked* away their precious remaining seconds together, the lights of Monaco glittering through the open French doors, the Cote d'Azur providing a breathtaking vista. Who wouldn't want to share this life with him? Why couldn't she just accept his proposal? She hated how his offer of marriage made her clench her gut in fear. She should be happy. Celebrating. This would be the easy answer to bringing up Eli together. They were best friends. Incredible lovers. Why not go with the flow? They could take a day to see Cannes with the baby, and she could snap pictures…savor the things she'd been too busy to notice in the early years of traveling with Elliot.

Yet something held her back. She couldn't push the word *yes* free. Every time she tried, her throat closed up. She trusted him…yet the thought of reliving the past eleven months again, of living without him…

Her fingers glided along his closely shorn hair. "You could have been killed that day your hair got singed."

"You're not going to get rid of me that easily," he said with a low chuckle and a stroke down her spine.

Ice chilled the blood in her veins at his words. "That wasn't funny."

"I'm just trying to lighten the mood." He angled back to kiss the tip of her nose, then look into her eyes. "I'm okay, Lucy Ann. Not a scratch on me that day."

She'd been in South Carolina when it had happened, her belly swelling with his child and her heart heavy with the decision of when to tell him about the baby. "That doesn't make it any less terrifying."

He grinned smugly. "You do care."

"Of course I care what happens to you. I always have. There's no denying our history, our friendship, how well we know each other." How could he doubt that, no matter what else they'd been through? "But I know something else. You're only interested in me now because I'm telling you no. You don't like being the one left behind."

Breathlessly, she finished her rant, stunned at herself. Her mouth had been ahead of her brain. She hadn't even realized she felt that way until the words came rolling out.

"That's not a very nice thing to say," he said tightly.

"But is it true?" She cupped his face.

He pulled her hands down gently and kissed both palms. "I already offered to stop racing. I meant it. I'm a father now and I understand that comes with respon- sibilities."

Responsibilities? Is that what they were to him? But then, in a way, that's what she'd always been since he got out of reform school, since he'd offered her a job as his assistant even though at the time she hadn't been qualified for the job. He'd given it to her out of friend- ship—and, yes, the sense of obligation they felt to look out for each other.

That had been enough for a long time, more than either of them had gotten from anyone else in their lives. But right now with her heart in her throat, obligation didn't feel like nearly enough to build a life on.

She slid off him, the cooling breeze from the fan chill- ing her bared flesh. "Do whatever you want."

"What did I say wrong? You want me to quit and I offer and now you're angry?"

"I didn't say I want you to quit." She opted for the sim- pler answer. "I understand how important your career is to you. You have a competitive nature and that's not a bad thing. It's made you an incredibly successful man."

"You mentioned my competitiveness earlier. Lucy Ann, that's not why I—"

She rolled to her side and pressed her fingers to his mouth before he could get back to the proposal subject again. "You've channeled your edginess and your drive to win. That's not a bad thing." She tapped his bottom lip. "Enough talk. You should rest up now so you're fo- cused for the race."

And so she could escape to her room, away from the building temptation to take what he offered and worry about the consequences later. Except with Elliot's mus- cled arm draped over her waist, she couldn't quite bring herself to move out of his embrace. His hand moved along her back soothingly. Slowly, her body began to relax, melting into the fantastic mattress.

"Lucy Ann? You're right, you know." Elliot's words were so low she almost didn't hear him.

"Right about what?" she asked, groggy, almost asleep.

"I like to win— Wait. Scratch that. I *need* to win."

Opening her eyes, she didn't move, just stared at his chest and listened. There was no escaping this conversation. Wherever it led them.

"There are two kinds of people in the world. Ones who have known physical pain and those who never will. Being beaten…" He swallowed hard, his heart hammering so loudly she could feel her pulse sync up with his, racing, knowing just what that word *beating* meant to him growing up. "That does something to your soul. Changes you. You can heal. You can move on. But you're forever changed by that moment you finally break, crying for it to stop."

His voice stayed emotionless, but what he said sliced through her all the more because of the steely control he forced on himself.

Her hand fluttered to rest on his heart as she pressed a kiss to his shoulder. "Oh, God, Elliot—"

"Don't speak. Not yet." He linked his fingers with hers. "The thing is, we all like to think we're strong enough to hold out when that person brings on the belt, the shoe, the branch, or hell, even a hand used as a weapon. And there's a rush in holding out at first, deluding yourself into believing you can actually win."

She willed herself to stay completely still, barely breathing, while he poured out the truth she'd always known. She'd even seen the marks he'd refused to acknowledge. Hearing him talk about it, though, shredded her heart, every revelation making her ache for what he'd suffered growing up. She also knew he wouldn't accept her sympathy now any more than he had then. So she gave him the only thing she could—total silence while he spoke.

"The person with the weapon is after one thing," he shared, referring to his father in such a vague sense as if that gave him distance, protection. "It isn't actually about the pain. It's about submission."

She couldn't hold back the flinch or a whimper of sympathy.

Elliot tipped her chin until she looked at him. "But you see, it's okay now. When I'm out there racing, it's my chance to win. No one, not one damn soul, will ever beat me again."

She held her breath, wrestling with what to do next, how they could go forward. This wasn't the time to pledge futures, but it also wasn't the time to walk away. Growing up, she'd always known how to be there for him. At this moment, she didn't have a clue.

The squawk of their son over the nursery monitor jolted them both. And she wasn't sure who was more relieved.

Her or Elliot.

Elliot barely tasted the gourmet brunch catered privately at a crowded café near the race day venue. With two hundred thousand people pouring into the small principality for the circuit's most famous event, there were fans and media everywhere. At least his friends and mentor seemed to be enjoying themselves. He wanted to chalk up his lack of enthusiasm to sleep deprivation.

Race day in Monaco had always been one of Elliot's favorites, from the way the sun glinted just right off the streets to the energy of the crowds. The circuit was considered one of the most challenging Formula One routes—narrow roads, tight turns and changing elevations made it all the more exciting, edgy, demanding.

And just that fast, Lucy Ann's words haunted him, how she'd accused him of searching out challenges. How she'd accused him of seeing her as a challenge. Damn it all, he just wanted them to build a future together.

What would she be thinking, sitting in the stands today with his school friends and their wives?

He glanced at her across the table, strain showing in the creases along her forehead and the dark smudges under her eyes. He wanted to take Eli from her arms so she could rest, but wasn't sure if she would object. He didn't want to cause a scene or upset her more.

With a mumbled excuse, he scraped back his chair and left the table. He needed air. Space.

He angled his way out of the room—damn, he had too many curious friends these days—and into the deserted patio garden in the back. All the patrons had flocked out front to the street side to watch the crowds already claiming their places to watch the race. But back here, olive trees and rosebushes packed the small space so densely he almost didn't see his old high school headmaster—now an Interpol handler—sitting on a bench sending text messages.

Colonel Salvatore sat beside his preteen son, who was every bit as fixated on his Game Boy as his father was on his phone. A couple of empty plates rested between them.

How had he missed them leaving the table? Damn, his mind wasn't where it was supposed to be.

Colonel Salvatore stood, mumbled something to his son, then walked toward Elliot without once looking up from his phone. The guy always had been the master of multitasking. Very little slipped by him. Ever.

The older man finally tucked away his cell phone and nodded. "We couldn't sit still," he said diplomatically, "so we're out here playing 'Angry Monkeys' or something like that."

"I'm sure you both enjoyed the food more here where it's quieter," he said diplomatically. "I could sure use parenting advice if you've got some to offer up."

Salvatore straightened his standard red tie. He wore the same color gray suit as always, like a retirement uniform. "Why don't you ask the guys inside?"

"They only have babies. They're new parents." Like him. Treading water as fast as he could and still choking. "You have an older boy."

"A son I rarely see due to my work schedule." He winced. "So again I say, I'm not the one to help."

"Then your first piece of advice would be for me to spend time with him."

"I guess it would." He glanced over at his son, whose thumbs were flying over the buttons. "Gifts don't make up for absence. Although don't underestimate the power of a well-chosen video game."

"Thank God we have the inside scoop with Troy's latest inventions." Maybe that's who he needed to be talking to. Maybe Troy could invent a baby app. Elliot shoved a hand over his hair, realizing how ridiculous the thought sounded. He must be sleep-deprived. "I'm a little short on role models in the father department—other than you."

Salvatore's eyebrows went up at the unexpected compliment. "Um, uh, thank you," he stuttered uncharacteristically.

"Advice then?"

"Don't screw up."

"That's it?" Elliot barked. "Don't screw up?"

"Fine, I'll spell it out for you." Salvatore smiled as if

he'd been toying with him all along. Then the grin faded. "You've had to steal everything you've ever wanted in life. From food to cars to friends—to your freedom."

"I'm past that."

"Are you?" The savvy Interpol handler leaned against the centuries-old brick wall, an ivy trellis beside him. "It's difficult for me to see beyond the boy you were when you arrived at my school as a teenager hell-bent on self-destructing."

"Self-destructing?" he said defensively. "I'm not sure I follow." He was all about winning.

"You stole that car on purpose to escape your father, and you feel guilty as hell for leaving Lucy Ann behind," Salvatore said so damn perceptively he might as well have been listening in on Elliot's recent conversations. "You expected to go to jail as punishment and since that didn't happen, you've been trying to prove to the world just how bad you are. You pushed Lucy Ann away by getting engaged to Gianna."

"When did you find time to get your psychology degree between being a headmaster and an Interpol handler?"

"There you go again, trying to prove what a smart-ass you are."

Damn it. Didn't it suck to realize how well he played to type? He took a steadying breath and focused.

"I'm trying to do the right thing by Lucy Ann now. I want to live up to my obligations."

"The right thing." The colonel scratched a hand over gray hair buzzed as short of Elliot's. "What is that?"

"Provide for our son… Marry her… Damn it, colonel, clearly you think I'm tanking here. Is it fun watching me flounder?"

"If I tell you what to do, you won't learn a thing. A

mentor guides, steers. Think of it as a race," he said with a nod—which Elliot knew from years in the man's office meant this conversation was over. Colonel Salvatore fished out his phone and headed back to sit silently beside his son.

Elliot pinched the bridge of his nose and pivoted toward the iron gate that led to the back street. He needed to get his head on straight before the race. Hell, he needed to get his head back on straight, period. Because right now, he could have sworn he must be hallucinating.

Beyond the iron gate, he saw a curly-haired brunette who looked startlingly like his former fiancée. He narrowed his eyes, looking closer, shock knocking him back a step as Gianna crossed the street on the arm of a Brazilian Formula One champion.

Lucy Ann usually found race day exciting, but she couldn't shake the feeling of impending doom. The sense that she and Elliot weren't going to figure out how to make things work between them before the end of their time together. Thank goodness Mrs. Clayworth had taken the baby back to the condo to nap, because Lucy Ann was beyond distracted.

Sitting in the private viewing box with Elliot's friends and the relatives of other drivers, she tried to stifle her fears, to reassure herself that she and Elliot could find a way to parent together—possibly even learn to form a relationship as a couple. That she could figure out how to heal the wounds from his past, which still haunted everything he did.

The buzz of conversation increased behind her, a frenzy of whispers and mumbles in multiple languages. She turned away from the viewing window and monitors broadcasting prerace hubbub, newscasters speaking in French, English, Spanish and a couple of languages she didn't recognize. She looked past the catering staff carrying glasses of champagne to the entrance. A gasp caught in her throat.

Gianna? Here?

The other woman worked her way down the steps, her dark curls bouncing. Shock, followed by a burst of anger, rippled through Lucy Ann as she watched Gianna stride confidently closer. Her white dress clung to her teeny-tiny body. Clearly those hips had never given birth. And Lucy Ann was long past her days of wearing anything white thanks to baby spit-up. Not that she would trade her son for a size-zero figure and a closet full of white clothes.

Above all, she did not want a scene in front of the media. Gianna's eyes were locked on her, her path determined. If the woman thought she could intimidate, she was sorely mistaken.

Lucy Ann shot to her feet and marched up the stairs, her low heels clicking. She threw her arms wide and said loud enough for all to hear, "Gianna, so glad you could make it."

Stunned, the woman almost tripped over her own stilettos. "Um, I—"

Lucy Ann hugged her hard and whispered in her ear, "We're going to have a quick little private chat and, above all, we will not cause a scene before the race."

She knew how fast gossip spread and she didn't intend to let any negative energy ripple through the crowd. And she definitely didn't intend for anyone to see her lose her calm. She hauled the other woman down the hall and into a ladies' room, locking the door behind them.

Once she was sure no one else was in the small sitting area or in the stalls, she confronted Elliot's former fiancée. "Why are you here?"

Gianna shook her curls. "I'm here with a retired Brazilian racer. I was simply coming by to say hello."

"I'm not buying that." Lucy Ann stared back at the other woman and found she wasn't jealous so much as angry that someone was trying mess with her happiness—hers, Elliot's and Eli's.

The fake smile finally faded from Gianna's face. "I came back because now it's a fair fight."

At least the woman wasn't denying it. "I'm not sure I follow your logic."

"Before, when I found out about you and the baby—"

Lucy gasped. "You knew?"

"I found out by accident. I got nosy about you, looked into your life…" She shrugged. "I was devastated, but I broke off the engagement."

"Whoa, hold on." Lucy Ann held up a hand. "I don't understand. Elliot said you broke up because of his Interpol work. That you couldn't handle the danger."

She rolled her dramatic Italian eyes. "Men are so very easy to deceive. I broke the engagement because I couldn't be the one to tell him about your pregnancy. I couldn't be 'that' woman. The one who broke up true love. The evil one in the triangle. But I also couldn't marry him knowing he might still want you or his child."

"So you left." Lucy Ann's legs gave way and she sagged back against the steel door.

"I loved him enough to leave and let him figure this out on his own."

If she'd really loved him, Gianna would have told him about his child, but then Lucy Ann figured who was she to throw stones on that issue? "Do you still love Elliot?"

"Yes, I do."

She searched the woman's eyes and saw…genuine heartache. "You're not at all what I expected."

Gianna's pouty smile faltered. "And you're everything I feared."

So where did they go from here? That question hammered through Lucy Ann's mind so loudly it took her a moment to realize the noise was real. Feet drummed overhead with the sound of people running. People screaming?

She looked quickly at Gianna, whose eyes were already widening in confusion, as well. Lucy Ann turned on her heels, unlocked the door and found mass confusion. Spectators and security running. Reporters rushing with their cameras at the ready, shouting questions and directions in different languages.

Lucy Ann grabbed the arm of a passing guard. "What's going on?"

"Ma'am, there's been an accident in the lineup. Please return to your seat and let us do our jobs," the guard said hurriedly and pulled away, melting into the crowd.

"An accident?" Her stomach lurched with fear.

There were other drivers. Many other drivers. And an accident while lining up would be slow? Right? Unless someone was doing a preliminary warm-up lap.... So many horrifying scenarios played through her mind, all of them involving Elliot. She shoved into the crush, searching for a path through to her viewing area or to the nearest telecast screen. Finally, she spotted a wide-screen TV mounted in a corner, broadcasting images of flames.

The words scrolling across the bottom blared what she already knew deep in her terrified heart.

Elliot had crashed.

Twelve

Her heart in her throat, Lucy Ann pushed past Gianna and shouldered through the bustling crush of panicked observers. She reached into her tailored jacket and pulled out her pass giving her unlimited access. She couldn't just sit in the private viewing area and wait for someone to call her. What if Elliot needed her? She refused to accept the possibility that he could be dead. Even the word made her throat close up tight.

Her low pumps clicked on the stairs as she raced through various checkpoints, flashing the access pass every step of the way.

Finally, thank God, finally, she ran out onto the street level where security guards created an impenetrable wall. The wind whipped her yellow sundress around her legs as she sprinted. Her pulse pounding in her ears, she searched the lanes of race cars, looking for flames. But she found no signs of a major explosion.

A siren's wail sliced through her. An ambulance navigated past a throng of race personnel spraying down the street with fire extinguishers. The vehicle moved toward two race cars, one on its side, the other sideways as if it had spun out into a skid. As much as she wanted to deny what her eyes saw, the car on its side belonged to Elliot.

Emergency workers crawled all over the vehicle, prying open the door. Blinking back burning tears, Lucy Ann strained against an arm holding her back, desperate to see. Her shouts were swallowed up in the roar of activity until she couldn't even hear her own incoherent pleas.

The door flew open, and her breath lodged somewhere in her throat. She couldn't breathe, gasp or shout. Just wait.

Rescue workers reached inside, then hauled Elliot out. Alive.

She sagged against the person behind her. She glanced back to find Elliot's Interpol handler, Colonel Salvatore, at her side. He braced her reassuringly, his eyes locked on the battered race car. Elliot was moving, slowly but steadily. The rescue workers tried to keep his arms over their shoulders so they could walk him to a waiting ambulance. But he shook his head, easing them aside and standing on his own two feet. He pulled off his helmet and waved to the crowd, signaling that all was okay.

The crowd roared, a round of applause thundering, the reverberations shuddering through her along with her relief. His gaze homed in on her. Lucy Ann felt the impact all the way to her toes. Elliot was alive. Again and again, the thought echoed through her mind in a continual loop of reassurance, because heaven help her, she loved him. Truly loved him. That knowledge rolled through her, settled into her, in a fit that told her what she'd known all along.

They'd always loved each other.

At this moment, she didn't doubt that he loved her back. No matter what problems, disagreements or betrayals they might have weathered, the bond was there. She wished she could rejoice in that, but the fear was still rooted deep inside her, the inescapable sense of foreboding.

Elliot pushed past the emergency personnel and... heaven only knew who else because she couldn't bring herself to look at anyone except Elliot walking toward her, the scent of smoke tingling in her nose as the sea breeze blew in. The sun shone down on the man she loved, bright Mediterranean rays glinting off the silver trim on his racing gear with each bold step closer.

She vaguely registered the colonel flashing some kind of badge that had the security cop stepping aside and letting her stumble past. She regained her footing and sprinted toward Elliot.

"Thank God you're okay." Slamming into his chest, she wrapped her arms around him.

He kissed her once, firmly, reassuringly, then walked her away from the sidelines, the crowd parting, or maybe someone made the path for them. She couldn't think of anything but the man beside her, the warmth of him, the sound of his heartbeat, the scent of his aftershave and perspiration.

Tears of relief streaming down her face, she didn't bother asking where they were going. She trusted him, the father of her child, and honestly didn't care where they went as long as she could keep her hands on him, her cheek pressed to his chest, the fire-retardant material of his uniform bristly against her skin. He pushed through a door into a private office. She didn't care whose or how he'd chosen the stark space filled with only a wooden desk, a black leather sofa and framed racing photos.

Briskly, he closed and locked the door. "Lucy Ann, deep breaths or you're going to pass out. I'm okay." His voice soothed over her in waves. "It was just a minor accident. The other guy's axle broke and he slammed into me. Everyone's fine."

She swiped her wrists over her damp eyes, undoubtedly smearing mascara all over her face. "When there's smoke—possibly fire—involved, I wouldn't call that minor."

Elliot cradled her face in his gloved hands. "My hair didn't even get singed."

"I'm not in a joking mood." She sketched jerky hands over him, needing to touch him.

"Then help me out." He stalled one of her hands and kissed her palm. "What can I say to reassure you?"

"Nothing," she decided. "There's nothing to say right now."

It was a time for action.

She tugged her hand free and looped her arms around his neck again and drew his face down to hers. She kissed him. More than a kiss. A declaration and affirmation that he was alive. She needed to connect with him, even if only on a physical level.

"Lucy Ann," he muttered against her mouth, "are you sure you know what you're doing?"

"Are you planning to go back to the race?" she asked, gripping his shoulders.

"My car's in no shape to race. You know that. But are you cert—"

She kissed him quiet. She was so tired of doubts and questions and reservations. Most of all, she couldn't bear for this to be about the past anymore. To feel more pain for him. For herself. For how damn awful their child-hoods had been—his even worse than hers.

Hell, she'd lived through those years with him, doing her best to protect him by taking the brunt of the blame when she could. But when the adults wouldn't step up and make things right, there was only so much a kid could do.

They weren't children any longer, but she still couldn't stand to think of him getting hurt in any way. She would do anything to keep danger away, to make them both forget everything.

At this moment, that "anything" involved mind-blowing sex against the door. Fast and intense. No fun games or pretty fairy tales. This was reality.

She tugged at his zipper, and he didn't protest this time. He simply drew back long enough to tug his racing gloves off with his teeth. With her spine pressed to the door, he bunched up her silky dress until a cool breeze blew across her legs. A second later, he twisted and snapped her panties free, the scrap of lace giving way to him as fully as she did.

But she took as much as she gave. She nudged the zipper wider, nudging his uniform aside until she released his erection, steely and hot in her hand. Then, he was inside her.

Her head thunked against the metal panel, her eyes sliding closed as she lost herself in sensation. She glided a foot along his calf, up farther until her leg hitched around him, drawing him deeper, deeper in a frenzied meeting of their bodies.

All too soon, the pleasure built to a crescendo, a wave swelling on the tide of emotions, fear and adrenaline. And yes, love. She buried her face in his shoulder, trying to hold back the shout rolling up her throat. His hoarse encouragement in her ear sent pleasure crashing over her. Feeling him tense in her arms, shudder with his own completion, sent a fresh tingle of aftershocks through her. Her body clamped around him in an instinctive need to keep him with her.

With each panting breath, she drew in the scent of them. His forehead fell to rest against the door, her fingers playing with the close-shorn hair at the base of his neck. Slowly, her senses allowed in the rest of the world, the dim echo outside reminding her they couldn't hide in here forever.

They couldn't hide from the truth any longer.

Even as she took him now, felt the familiar draw of this man she'd known for as long as she could remember, she also realized she didn't belong here in this world now. She couldn't keep him because she couldn't stay.

No matter how intrinsic the connection and attraction between them, this wasn't the life she'd dreamed of when they'd built those fairy-tale forts and castles. In her fantasies, they'd all just looked like a real home. A safe haven.

She loved him. She always had. But she'd spent most of her adult life following him. It was time to take charge of her life, for herself and for her son.

It was time to go home.

As Elliot angled back and started to smile at her, she captured his face in her hands and shook her head.

"Elliot, I can't do this anymore, trying to build a life on fairy tales. I need something more, a real life, and maybe that sounds boring to you, but I know who I am now. I know the life I want to live and it isn't here."

His eyes searched hers, confused and a little angry. "Lucy Ann—"

She pressed her fingers to his mouth. "I don't want

to argue with you. Not like last time. We can't do that to each other again—or to Eli."

He clasped her hand, a pulse throbbing double time in his neck. "Are you sure there's nothing I can do to change your mind?"

God, she wanted to believe he could, but right now with the scent of smoke clinging to his clothes and the adrenaline still crackling in the air, she couldn't see any other way. "No, Elliot. I'm afraid not."

Slowly, he released her hand. His face went somber, resigned. He understood her in that same perfect and tragic way she understood him. He already knew.

They'd just said goodbye.

The next day, Elliot didn't know how he was going to say goodbye. But the time had come. He sat on Aunt Carla's front porch swing while Lucy Ann fed Eli and put him down for a nap.

God, why couldn't he and Lucy Ann have had some massive argument that made it easier to walk away, like before?

Instead, there had been this quiet, painful realization that she was leaving him. No matter how many fairy-tale endings he tried to create for her, she'd seen through them all. After their crazy, out-of-control encounter against the door, they'd returned to the hotel. She'd packed. He'd arranged for his private jet to fly them home to South Carolina.

Lucy Ann had made a token offer to travel on her own, not to disrupt his schedule—not to distract him. The implication had been there. The accident had happened because his life was fracturing. He couldn't deny it.

But he'd damn well insisted on bringing them back here himself.

The front door creaked open, and he looked up sharply. Lucy Ann's aunt walked through. He sagged back in his swing, relieved to have the inevitable farewell delayed for a few more minutes. He knew Lucy Ann would let him be a part of his son's world, but this was not how he wanted their lives to play out.

Carla settled next to him on the swing, her T-shirt appliquéd with little spring chickens. "Glad to know you survived in one piece."

"It was a minor accident," he insisted again, the wind rustling the oak trees in time with the groan of the chains holding the swing. The scent of Carolina jasmine reminded him of Lucy Ann.

"I meant that kidnapping stunt your friends staged. Turning your whole life upside down."

Right now, it didn't feel like he'd walked away unscathed. The weight on his chest pressed heavier with every second, hadn't let up since he'd been pulled from his damaged car. "I'll provide for Lucy Ann and Eli."

"That was never in question." She patted his knee. "I'm glad you got out of here all those years ago."

"I thought you wanted Lucy Ann to stay? That's always been my impression over the years."

"I do believe she belongs here. But we're not talking about her." She folded her arms over the row of cheerful chickens. "I'm talking about what you needed as a teenager. You had to leave first before you could find any peace here. Although, perhaps it was important for Lucy Ann to leave for a while, as well."

There was something in her voice—a kindred spirit? An understanding? Her life hadn't been easy either, and he found himself saying, "You didn't go."

"I couldn't. Not when Lucy Ann needed me. She was my one shot at motherhood since I couldn't have kids of my own." She shrugged. "Once she left with you, I'd already settled in. I'm on my own now."

"I just assumed you didn't want kids." He was realizing how little time he'd spent talking to this woman who'd given him safe harbor, the woman who'd been there for Lucy Ann and Eli. He didn't have much in the way of positive experience with blood relatives, but it was undoubtedly time to figure that out.

"I would have adopted," Carla confided, "but my husband had a record. Some youthful indiscretions with breaking and entering. Years later it didn't seem like it should have mattered to the adoption agencies that he'd broken into the country club to dump a bunch of Tootsie Rolls in the pool."

Elliot grinned nostalgically. "Sounds like he would have made a great addition to the Alpha Brotherhood."

And might Elliot have found a mentor with Lucy Ann's uncle as well if he'd taken the time to try?

"I wish Lucy Ann could have had those kinds of friendships for herself. She was lost after you left," Carla said pointedly. "She didn't find her confidence until later."

What was she talking about? "Lucy Ann is the strongest, most confident person I've ever met. I wouldn't have made it without her."

He looked into those woods and thought about the dream world she'd given him as a kid, more effective an escape than even his favorite book.

"You protected her, but always saw her strengths. That's a wonderful thing." Carla pinned him with unrelenting brown eyes much like her stubborn niece's. "But you also never saw her vulnerabilities or insecurities. She's not perfect, Elliot. You need to stop expecting her to be your fairy-tale princess and just let her be human."

What the hell was she talking about? He didn't have time to ask because she pushed up from the swing and left him sitting there, alone. Nothing but the creak of the swing and the rustle of branches overhead kept him company. There was so much noise in this ends-of-the-earth place.

Carla's words floated around in his brain like dust searching for a place to land. Damn it all, he knew Lucy Ann better than anyone. He saw her strengths and yes, her flaws, too. Everyone had flaws. He didn't expect her to be perfect. He loved her just the way she—

He loved her.

The dust in his brain settled. The world clarified, taking shape around those three words. He loved her. It felt so simple to acknowledge, he wondered why he hadn't put the form to their relationship before. Why hadn't he just told her?

The trees swayed harder in the wind that predicted a storm. He couldn't remember when he'd ever told anyone he loved them. But he must have, a long time ago. Kids told their parents they loved them. Although now that he thought about it, right there likely laid the answer for why the word *love* had dried up inside him.

He'd told himself he wanted to be a better parent than his father—a better man than his father. Now he realized being a better man didn't have a thing to do with leaving this porch or this town. Running away didn't change him. This place had never been the problem.

He had been the problem. And the time had come to make some real changes in himself, changes that would make him the father Eli deserved. Changes that would make him the man Lucy Ann deserved.

Finally, he understood how to build their life together.

* * *

The time was rapidly approaching to say goodbye to Elliot.

Her mind full of regrets and second thoughts, Lucy Ann rocked in the old bentwood antique in her room at Carla's, Eli on her shoulder. She held him to comfort herself since he'd long since settled into a deep sleep. She planned to find a place of her own within the next two weeks, no leaning on her aunt this time.

The past day since they'd left Monte Carlo after the horrifying accident had zipped by in such a haze of pain and worry. Her heart still hadn't completely settled into a steady beat after Elliot's accident. Right up to the last second, she'd hoped he would come up with a Hail Mary plan for them to build a real life together for Eli. She loved Elliot with all her heart, but she couldn't deny her responsibilities to her son. He needed a stable life.

To be honest, so did she.

There was a time she'd dreamed of escaping simple roots like the cabin in the woods, and now she saw the value of the old brass bed that had given her a safe place to slip away. The Dutch doll quilt draped over the footboard had been made for her by her aunt for her eighth birthday. She soaked in the good memories and the love in this place now, appreciating them with new eyes—but still that didn't ease the unbearable pain in her breaking heart as she hoped against all hope for a last-minute solution.

Footsteps sounded in the hall—even, manly and familiar. She would recognize the sound of Elliot anywhere. She had only a second to blink back the sting of tears before the door opened.

Elliot filled the frame, his broad-shouldered body that of a mature man, although in faded jeans and a simple gray T-shirt, he looked more like *her* Elliot. As if this weren't already difficult enough.

She smoothed a hand along Eli's back, soaking in more comfort from his baby-powder-fresh scent. "Did you want to hold him before you go?"

"Actually, I thought you and I could go for a walk first and talk about our future," he said, his handsome face inscrutable.

What else could there be left to say? She wasn't sure her heart could take any more, although another part of her urged her to continue even through the ache, just to be with him for a few minutes longer.

"Sure," she answered, deciding he must want to discuss visitation with Eli. She wouldn't keep him from his son. She'd made a horrible mistake in delaying telling Elliot for even a day. She owed him her cooperation now. "Yes, we should talk about the future, but before we do that, I need to know where you stand with Gianna. She approached me at the stadium just before your wreck." The next part was tougher to share but had to be addressed. "She said she's still in love with you."

His forehead furrowed. "I'm sorry you had to go through that, but let's be very clear. I do *not* love Gianna and I never did, not really. I did her a grave injustice by rebounding into a relationship with her because I was hurting over our breakup." The carefully controlled expression faded and honest emotion stamped itself clearly in his eyes. "That's a mistake I will not repeat. She is completely in the past. My future is with you and Eli. Which is what I want to speak with you about. Now, can we walk?"

"Of course," she said, relief that one hurdle was past and that she wouldn't have to worry about Gianna popping up in their lives again.

Standing, Lucy Ann placed her snoozing son in his portable crib set up beside her bed. She felt Elliot behind her a second before he smoothed a hand over their son's head affectionately, then turned to leave.

Wordlessly, she followed Elliot past the Hummel collection and outside, striding beside him down the porch steps, toward a path leading into the woods. Funny how she knew without hesitation this was where they would walk, their same footpath and forest hideout from their childhood years. Oak trees created a tunnel arch over the dappled trail, jasmine vines climbing and blooming. Gray and orange shadows played hide-and-seek as the sunset pushed through the branches. Pine trees reached for the sky. She'd forgotten how peaceful this place was.

Of course she also knew she'd walked the same course over the past year searching for this peace. Elliot's presence brought the moment to shimmering life as he walked beside her, his hands in his pockets. She assumed he had a destination in mind since they still weren't talking. A dozen steps later they came around a bend and—

Four of her aunt's quilts were draped over the branches, creating a fort just like the ones they'd built in the past. Another blanket covered the floor of their forest castle.

Lucy Ann gasped, surprised. Enchanted. And so moved that fresh tears stung her eyes.

Elliot held out a hand and she took it. The warmth and familiarity of his touch wrapped around her, seeping into her veins. She wasn't sure where he was going with this planned conversation, but she knew she couldn't turn back. She needed to see it through and prayed that somehow he'd found a way for them all to be together.

He guided her to their fort, and she sat cross-legged, her body moving on instinct from hundreds of similar hideaways here. He took his place beside her, no fancy trappings but no less beautiful than the places they'd traveled.

"Elliot, I hope you know that I am so very sorry for not telling you about Eli sooner," she said softly, earnestly. "If I had it to do over again, I swear to you I would handle things differently. I know I can't prove that, but I mean it—"

He covered her hand with his, their fingers linking. "I believe you."

The honesty in his voice as he spoke those three words healed something inside her she hadn't realized was hurting until now. "Thank you, Elliot. Your forgiveness means more to me than I can say."

His chest rose and fell with a deep sigh. "I'm done with racing. There's no reason to continue putting my life at risk in the car—or with Interpol, for that matter."

The declaration made her selfishly want to grasp at what he offered. But she knew forcing him into the decision would backfire for both of them. "Thank you for offering again, but as I said before, I don't want you to make that sacrifice for me. I don't want you to do something that's going to make you unhappy, because in the end that's not going to work for either of us—"

"This isn't about you. It isn't even about Eli, although I would do anything for either of you." He squeezed her fingers until she looked into his eyes. "This decision is about me. Interpol has other freelancers to call upon. I mean it when I say I'm through with the racing circuit. I don't need the money, the notoriety. The risk or the chaos. I have everything I want with you and Eli."

"But please know I'm not asking that sacrifice from you." Although, oh, God, it meant so much to her that he'd offered.

He lifted her hand and kissed the inside of her wrist.

"Being with you isn't a sacrifice. Having you, I gain everything."

Seeing the forgiveness that flooded his eyes, so quickly, without hesitation, she realized for the first time how much more difficult her deception must have been for him, given his past. All his life he'd been let down by people who were supposed to love him and protect him. His father had beaten him and for years he'd taken it to shield his mother. His mother hadn't protected him. Beyond that, his mother had walked out, leaving him behind. On the most fundamental levels, he'd been betrayed. He'd spent most of his adult years choosing relationships with women that were destined to fail.

And when their friendship moved to a deeper level, he'd self-destructed again by staying away. He'd been just as scared as she was about believing in the connection they'd shared the night they'd made love.

She knew him so well, yet she'd turned off all her intuition about him and run.

"Life doesn't have to be about absolutes. Your world or my world, a castle or a fort. There are ways to compromise."

Hope flared in his green eyes. "What are you suggesting?"

"You can have me." She slid her arms around his neck. "Even if we're apart for some of the year, we can make that work. We don't have to follow you every day, but Eli and I can still travel."

"I know you didn't ask me to give it up," he interrupted. "But it's what I want—a solid base for our son and any other children we have. I'm done running away. It's time for us to build a home. We've been dreaming of this since we tossed blankets over branches in the forest as kids. Lucy Ann," he repeated, "it's time for me to come home and make that dream come true. I love you, Lucy Ann, and I want you to be my wife."

How could she do anything but embrace this beautiful future he'd just offered them both? Her heart's desire had come true. And now, she was ready, she'd found her strength and footing, to be partners with this man for life.

"I've loved you all my life, Elliot Starc. There is no other answer than yes. Yes, let's build our life together, a fairy tale on our own terms."

The sigh of relief that racked his body made her realize he'd been every bit as afraid of losing this chance. She pressed her lips to his and sealed their future together as best friends, lovers, soul mates.

He swept back her hair and said against her mouth, "Right here, on this spot, let's build that house."

"Here?" She appreciated the sacrifice he was making, returning here to a town with so many ghosts and working to find peace. "What if we take our blankets and explore the South Carolina coast together until we find the perfect spot—a place with a little bit of home, but a place that's also new to us where we can start fresh."

"I like the way you dream, Lucy Ann. Sounds perfect." He smiled with happiness and a newfound peace. "We'll build that home, a place for our son to play, and if we have other children, where they can all grow secure." He looked back at her, love as tangible in his eyes as those dreams for their future. "What do you think?"

"I believe you write the most amazing happily ever after ever."

Epilogue

Elliot Starc had faced danger his whole life. First at the hands of his heavy-fisted father. Later as a Formula One race car driver who used his world travels to feed information to Interpol.

But he'd never expected to be kidnapped. Especially not in the middle of his son's second birthday party.

Apparently, about thirty seconds ago, one of his friends had snuck up behind him and tied a bandanna over his eyes. He wasn't sure who since he could only hear a bunch of toddlers giggling.

Elliot lost his bearings as two of his buddies turned him around, his deck shoes digging into the sand, waves rolling along the shore of his beach house. "Are we playing blind man's bluff or pin the tail on the donkey?"

"Neither." The breeze carried Lucy Ann's voice along with her jasmine scent. "We're playing guess this object."

Something fuzzy and stuffed landed in his hands.

Some kind of toy maybe? He frowned, no clue what he held, which brought more laughter from his Alpha Brotherhood buddies who'd all gathered here with their families. Thank goodness he and Lucy Ann had plenty of room in their home and the guest house.

He'd bought beach property on a Low Country Carolina island, private enough to attract other celebrities who wanted normalcy in their lives. He and Lucy had built a house. Not as grand as he'd wanted to offer her, but he understood the place was a reflection of how they lived now. She'd scaled him back each step of the way on upgrades, reminding him of their new priorities. Their marriage and family topped the list—which meant no scrimping on space, even if he'd had to forgo a few extravagant extras.

As for upgrades, that money could be spent on other things. They'd started a scholarship foundation. Lucy Ann's organizational and promotional skills had the foundation running like clockwork, doubling in size. They'd kept to their plans to travel, working their schedule around his life, which had taken a surprising turn. Since he didn't have to worry about money, thanks to his investments, he'd started college, working toward a degree in English. He was studying the classics along with creative writing, and enjoying every minute of it. Lucy Ann had predicted he would one day be a college professor and novelist.

His wonderful wife was a smart woman and a big dreamer.

There was a lot to be said for focus. Although with each of the brothers focused on a different part of the world, they had a lot of ground covered. Colonel Salvatore had taught them well, giving them a firm foundation to build happy, productive lives even after their Interpol days were past.

Famous musician Malcolm Douglas and his wife were

currently sponsoring a charity tour with their children in tow, and if it went as well as they expected, it would be an annual affair. The Doctors Boothe had opened another clinic in Africa last month along with the Monte Carlo mega-rich Hughes family—their daughters along for the ribbon-cutting. Computer whiz Troy Donavan and his wife, Hillary, had a genius son who kept them both on their toes.

"Elliot." Lucy Ann's whisper caressed his ear. "You're not playing the game."

He peeled off his blindfold to find his beautiful wife standing in front of him. His eyes took in the sight of her in a yellow bikini with a crocheted cover-up. "I surrender."

She tucked her hand in his pocket and stole the toy from his hand, tucking it behind her back. "You're not getting off that easily."

Colonel Salvatore chuckled from a beach chair where he wore something other than his gray suit for once— gray swim trunks and T-shirt, but still. Not a suit. But they were all taking things easier these days. "You never did like to play by the rules."

Aunt Carla lifted a soda in toast from her towel under a beach umbrella. "I can attest to that."

Elliot reached toward Lucy Ann for the mysterious fuzzy toy. "Come on. Game over."

She backed up, laughing. "Catch me if you want it now."

She was light on her feet, and he still enjoyed the thrill of the chase when it came to his wife. Jogging a few yards before he caught her, Elliot swept her up into his arms and carried her behind a sand dune where he could kiss her properly as he'd been aching to do all day. Except his house was so full of friends and family.

With the waves crashing and sea grass rustling, Elliot kissed her as he'd done thousands of times and looked forward to doing thousands more until they drew their last breath. God, he loved this woman.

Slowly, he lowered her feet to the ground, and she molded her body to his. If there wasn't a party going on a few yards away, he would have taken this a lot further. Later, he promised himself, later he would bring her out to a cabana and make love to her with the sound of the ocean to serenade them—his studies in English and creative writing were making him downright poetic these days.

For now though, he had a mission. He caressed up her arm until he found her hand. With quick reflexes honed on the racetrack, he filched the mystery toy from her fingers. Although he had to admit, she didn't put up much of a fight.

He slid his hand back around, opened his fist and found…a baby toy. Specifically, a fuzzy yellow rabbit. "You're—"

"Pregnant," she finished the sentence with a shining smile. "Four weeks. I only just found out for sure."

They'd been trying for six months, and now their dream to give Eli a brother or a sister was coming true. He hugged her, lifting her feet off the ground and spinning her around.

Once her feet settled on the sand again, she said, "When we were kids, we dreamed of fairy tales. How funny that we didn't start believing them until we became adults."

His palm slid over her stomach. "Real life with you and our family beats any fairy tale, hands down."

* * * * *

COMING NEXT MONTH FROM

HARLEQUIN
Desire

Available February 4, 2014

#2281 HER TEXAN TO TAME

Lone Star Legacy • by Sara Orwig

The wide-open space of the Delaney's Texas ranch is the perfect place for chef Jessica to forget her past. But when the rugged ranch boss's flirtations become serious, the heat is undeniable!

#2282 WHAT A RANCHER WANTS

Texas Cattleman's Club: The Missing Mogul
by Sarah M. Anderson

Chance McDaniel knows what he wants when he sees it, and he wants Gabriella. But while this Texas rancher is skilled at seduction, he never expects the virginal Gabriella to capture his heart.

#2283 SNOWBOUND WITH A BILLIONAIRE

Billionaires and Babies • by Jules Bennett

Movie mogul Max Ford returns home, only to get snowed-in with his ex—and her baby! This time, Max will fight for the woman he lost—even as the truth tears them apart.

#2284 BACK IN HER HUSBAND'S BED

by Andrea Laurence

Nathan and his estranged wife, poker champion Annie, agree to play the happy couple to uncover cheating at his casino. But their bluff lands her back in her husband's bed—for good this time?

#2285 JUST ONE MORE NIGHT

The Pearl House • by Fiona Brand

Riveted by Elena's transformation from charming duckling into seriously sexy swan, Aussie Nick Messena wants one night with her. But soon Nick realizes one night will never be enough....

#2286 BOUND BY A CHILD

Baby Business • by Katherine Garbera

When their best friends leave them guardians of a baby girl, business rivals Allan and Jessi call a truce. But an unexpected attraction changes the terms of this merger.

YOU CAN FIND MORE INFORMATION ON UPCOMING HARLEQUIN® TITLES, FREE EXCERPTS AND MORE AT WWW.HARLEQUIN.COM.

HDCNM0114

SPECIAL EXCERPT FROM

 HARLEQUIN®

Desire

She ran from their marriage, but now she's returned to
Vegas and must play the happily married couple with her
estranged husband.

Here's a sneak peek at
BACK IN HER HUSBAND'S BED
by Andrea Laurence,
coming February 2014 from Harlequin® Desire!

Nate's brow furrowed, his eyes focused on her tightly clenched fist. "Put on the ring," he demanded softly.

Her heart skipped a beat in her chest. She'd sooner slip a noose over her head. That was how it felt, at least. Even back then. When she'd woken up the morning after the wedding with the platinum manacle clamped onto her, she'd popped a Xanax to stop the impending panic attack. She convinced herself that it would be okay, it was just the nerves of a new bride, but it didn't take long to realize she'd made a mistake.

Annie scrambled to find a reason not to put the ring on. She couldn't afford to start hyperventilating and give Nate the upper hand in any of this. Why did putting on a ring symbolic of nothing but a legally binding slip of paper bother her so much?

Nate frowned. He moved across the room with the stealthy grace of a panther, stopping just in front of her. Without speaking, he reached out and gripped her fist. One by one, he pried her fingers back and took the band from her.

She was no match for his firm grasp, especially when the surprising tingle of awareness traveled up her arm at his touch.

He held her left hand immobile, her heart pounding rapidly in her chest as the ring moved closer and closer.

"May I, Mrs. Reed?"

Her heart stopped altogether at the mention of her married name. Annie's breath caught in her throat as he pushed the band over her knuckle and nestled it snugly in place as he had at their wedding. His hot touch was in vast contrast to the icy cold metal against her skin. Although it fit perfectly, the ring seemed too tight. So did her shoes. On second thought, everything felt too tight. The room was too small. The air was too thin.

Annie's brain started swirling in the fog overtaking her mind. She started to tell Nate she needed to sit down, but it was too late.

Don't miss
BACK IN HER HUSBAND'S BED
by Andrea Laurence,
available February 2014 from
Harlequin® Desire wherever books are sold!

HARLEQUIN®
Desire

ALWAYS POWERFUL, PASSIONATE AND PROVOCATIVE.

Nothing's come easy to Chance McDaniel ever since his best friend
betrayed him. And when the deception explodes into a
Texas-size scandal, his best friend's sister, Gabriella del Toro, shows
up in town to pick up the pieces and capture his heart..

But will the web of deception her family has weaved ensnare
her yet again?

Look for **WHAT A RANCHER WANTS**
from Sarah M. Anderson next month
from Harlequin Desire!

Don't miss other scandalous titles from the
Texas Cattleman's Club miniseries, available now!

SOMETHING ABOUT THE BOSS
by Yvonne Lindsay

THE LONE STAR CINDERELLA
by Maureen Child

TO TAME A COWBOY
by Jules Bennett

IT HAPPENED ONE NIGHT
by Kathie DeNosky

BENEATH THE STETSON
by Janice Maynard

Available wherever books and ebooks are sold.

Powerful heroes…scandalous secrets…burning desires.

HD73295